THIS MATERIAL
RELEASED FOR P... SALE BY
EVERGREEN SCHOOL DISTRICT

8611029

F
Kel   Kelle... B....rly

The Minstrel

HEARTHWOOD ELEMENTARY SCHOOL
801 N. Elizabethwood Blvd.
Vancouver, Washington 98664

A Small, Elderly Dragon

BY BEVERLY KELLER

with pictures by Nola Langner Malone

LOTHROP, LEE & SHEPARD BOOKS
New York

8611029

King Wincealot

Text copyright © 1984 by Beverly Keller
Illustrations copyright © 1984 by Nola Langner
All rights reserved. No part of this book may be reproduced or utilized in
any form or by any means, electronic or mechanical, including photo-
copying, recording or by any information storage and retrieval system,
without permission in writing from the Publisher. Inquiries should be
addressed to Lothrop, Lee and Shepard Books, a division of William Mor-
row & Company, Inc., 105 Madison Avenue, New York, New York 10016.

Printed in the United States of America.
First Edition 1 2 3 4 5 6 7 8 9 10

Library of Congress Cataloging in Publication Data
Keller, Beverly. A small, elderly dragon.
SUMMARY: When the kingdom is overtaken by a sorcerer, young
Princess Dorma, nearsighted and awkward, helps a small, elderly dragon
find the power needed to save the villagers.
[1. Dragons—Fiction.
2. Princesses—Fiction. 3. Fantasy] I. Langer, Nola, ill. II. Title.
PZ7.K2813Sm 1984 [Fic] 83-13632 ISBN 0-688-02553-6

Design by Cecilia Yung

Volotor

Arnold
the high commissioner

MILES

Filene

Hugh

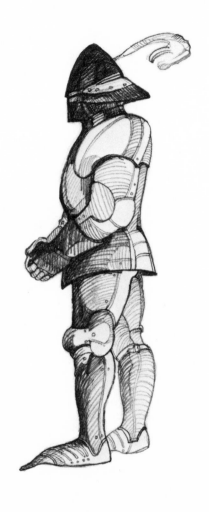

The Black Knight of Doom

Princess Dorma

For

MOTHER

and

DULCE

$\mathcal{W}$hile Minervia was not the largest or most prosperous of kingdoms, the Royal House of Wincealot had ruled it long enough to become attached to it.

one

E was beginning to have trouble with his hearing, and the fire from his nostrils, fire that once lit the horizon for miles around and seared whole rivers dry, was barely enough now to warm a corner of his lair. Sometimes on a winter night, curled with his dreadful jaws under his scaly tail, he shivered, partly from chill, partly from the thrill of recalling in dreams the bad old days when the mere rumor of his approach sent peasants yammering in terror.

He'd been a wicked dragon in his prime, and the people had taken great pride in him. He had stirred up more excitement in the kingdom than all its knights and nobles and natural disasters put together. After a dragon raid, nobody was expected to settle down as if nothing had happened. The only thing to do was take a holiday, get together to compare close calls, and have a little something for the nerves.

When tax collectors came down from the castle, the villagers would murmur, "Easy for you, up there surrounded by moat. You don't 'appen to live Right in the Path o' the Dragon."

When travelers from large, prosperous kingdoms came through expecting to be treated like royalty, it was a comfort to the peasants to say casually to one another, "Dragon did a deal o' damage to your place, did 'e, Wilfred?"

"Plowed up five acre wif 'is toenails. Toppled the forest not a stone's throw away."

"A terror, 'e is. I remember when 'e slithered down this very lane on 'is way to 'arass the palace. It was me brother 'arold came that close to bein' roasted 'ole."

" 'ere. See this mark? That's where I got cut by a bit o' flyin' boulder the time 'e tore up the quarry."

Then there were the youths and maidens. After every dragon tantrum, the villagers sacrificed ten of each. Since peasants were a practical lot, there was seldom any argument about who would be sacrificed. Sensitive maidens who were forever having their feelings hurt or complaining about sick headaches, strapping lads who were constantly brawling or talking up to their betters —somehow, everyone agreed, these seemed just right for the dragon.

There would be speeches, music, a little something to soothe the pangs. Then, with flowers tossed in their path, the twenty, all in white garments, would be taken to the monster's lair.

Almost.

A decent distance up the mountain, the villagers always broke and ran, leaving the sacrifices shivering on the path. After a bit, the doomed young would begin to bicker from sheer uneasiness, then to squabble, finally to brawl. It never occurred to them to run home. They knew they'd meet a cold welcome down below. They knew, too, that they'd meet their families, whom they'd disgraced by running home.

But what of the dragon?

Blystfylyl was his name, though nobody had taken the trouble to learn it.

He would wake after a rampage feeling miserable. Being a reptile, with all the failings of his kind, he couldn't bring himself to admit it was guilt he felt. He would lie in his cave, moaning, worrying that he was burning himself out, knowing that sooner or later he would have to do something about the sacrifices he was sure to find waiting below.

Maybe they've forgotten to send them this time, he'd think hopefully.

This was no comfort. While he was squeamish about humans, and shuddered to think of the *kind* that were always sent him, he had learned to expect them. Should the day come when they weren't there, he'd know he was no longer feared, or even respected. For a dragon, being taken lightly was even worse than youths and maidens.

When the sounds of young voices raised in yowling reached his lair, he would lumber out. Breathing a little fire over their heads to scare them speechless, he would herd his sacrifices into his den and then sweep it out hastily with his tail —he was sensitive about his slapdash housekeeping.

For a while, the conviction that he was going to devour them kept his hostages on their best behavior, but even their best was abominable. As the fear of being eaten faded, they began to act as if they were on vacation, scattering his belongings, complaining about the food, refusing to wash or to speak politely. When he wasn't tidying after them, or foraging for their feed, he sulked in crannies, yearning for a little privacy.

But the sacrifices would hang about for months until, in a fit of rebellion, or after an exchange of words with the sorely harried dragon, they'd run off one by one.

Anybody who had bothered to count would have found that every youth and maiden had come home in time, except for those who traveled abroad lecturing on The Horror of Dragons, and one who journeyed to the rim of the world and became a knight more fearsome than any beast.

However, since the young who came home were older and usually more civilized than when they left, nobody questioned a tradition that could hardly be improved.

The dragon, who had had human children on

his claws since the beginning of their species, became worn almost to a lizard by their care. As he grew older, he found it hard to summon the energy for his annual attack on the kingdom. He skipped a raid. Then another.

Finally, the last of his youths and maidens had been gone for years, and the tales they told had grown to the radiance of legend, rivaling in splendor even the old monster's dreams.

As time went by, however, and nothing was heard from the dragon, his prestige began to dwindle and the fear in which he was held ebbed. When half a decade passed without a rumble from him, tax collectors from the castle yawned at the same old stale tales about his forays. Visitors from large, rich kingdoms snickered at superstitious twaddle about the beast. What the old people called dragon snores was only thunder, what they called his stirring only earth tremors.

Of course, nobody offered to go up and see if there was still a dragon on the mountain. As silly a stunt as sleeping in a graveyard, the villagers agreed.

The kingdom of Minervia became so peaceful that visitors from other lands returned to vacation, then to retire. Some villagers made their homes into shops. Others set themselves up as tailors and pawnbrokers, attorneys and agents. A new inn was built.

HEARTHWOOD ELEMENTARY SCHOOL
801 N.E. Hearthwood Blvd.
Vancouver, Washington 98664

To make room for all this progress, ground was leveled, rivers dammed, trees felled.

Finally, the noise reached even the dragon's lair.

He stretched.

For a few weeks he scratched himself and listened.

At last, he lumbered out.

Far below him, thirty houses were being built.

He was shocked.

"Twenty," he roared, "twenty of their miserable young I would take at a time and give a decent home. But this is more than scales and fangs can bear. If they think they can send up thirty sacrifices without even the excuse of a raid, build nests for them right on my path . . ."

And he attacked, just as in the bad old days.

Almost.

His roar was more of a grumble. His fiery breath was barely enough to scorch a mountain. He was slow on his feet and short-winded.

But he managed. He managed to send all the workmen running and to squash a dozen houses. Then he had to crawl back to his lair and lie down with all his legs up.

The next day he felt miserable.

He groaned.

He piled cool boulders on his brow.

He waited for the sounds of young voices.

Silence.

20

He polished a few of his tail scales with his snout.

Silence.

Finally, muttering to keep his spirits up, he went to fetch his sacrifices.

There was not a youth. Not a maiden.

Only trampled houses, scattered rocks, and silence.

I gave this kingdom the worst years of my life, he thought, heartbroken. And now, in my twilight centuries, I'm forgotten. Scorned. Ignored.

Ignored.

This is the end, then. A dragon who is no longer respected has no reason for living.

Silently, as silently as is possible for a four-ton beast, he dragged himself back to his lair. Curling up, horrid jaws under armored tail, he shut his eyes to wait for the end, which might take five or ten years to arrive, the way dragons live and die.

two

O F course, he was wrong.

He was not being ignored.

There was a torrent of business at the inn that evening.

"D'ye remember the winter of ought-six, Albert? Picked up me ox, plow and all, 'e did, and left 'em standin' on me roof, neat as ye please."

"One flick of 'is tail cleared five acre o' me land that year. Swept it clean. I looked right up into 'is jaws. Right at the old forked tongue. 'Thank'ee, old fella,' says I, 'not that I'm sure ye meant it kindly.' "

" 'ere. See this mark . . ."

People gathered in the meeting hall to elect the youths and maidens for the sacrifice.

But soon sober thoughts began to surface,

22

for the village, remember, was in a state of progress.

"A 'oliday in the middle o' the week? Close up me shop just to see some sacrifices up to the dragon's?"

"Visitors want their meals, dragon or no."

"And 'oo 'as time for sewin' white garments to be worn only once?"

"It's the king should be protectin' us from the beast. Why can't 'e send it some spare lords and ladies? We're short-'anded enough down 'ere as it is."

And the villagers refused to send a soul.

The king was outraged. But his advisors persuaded him that attacking his own village would not be statesmanlike.

The Royal Dragon Commission was formed to hear witnesses, hold meetings, and prepare a report for the king.

"Just tell me about it, Arnold," he said to the high commissioner of the Royal Dragon Commission. "Don't make me read it."

The high commissioner of the Royal Dragon Commission, who was also the king's brother-in-law and chief advisor, narrowed his nostrils. He did not approve of the ruler entirely.

"Briefly," the high commissioner said, "we found the following: It has always been the custom to sacrifice twenty young to the dragon after each attack. But we strongly advise against the habit. First: It tends to encourage such raids. Second: By sending sacrifices we admit that: A: We have a dragon. B: We have no better way to deal with him. Fourth: This would have a bad effect on business."

King Wincealot, who was trying to retrace how the high commissioner had gotten from *B* to *Fourth,* realized an answer was expected. "What's the answer?"

"That comes next. Fifth: There must be a better answer."

Princess Dorma, the king's only child, came sweeping down the stairs, followed by a dozen twittering handmaidens.

"Must that girl keep sweeping down the stairs?" growled her father.

"Put down the broom, Dorma," her uncle Arnold told her sharply.

The handmaidens twittered out of sheer embarrassment. Like everybody, they had strong ideas about royalty: A princess should have blue eyes, long golden hair and fair skin, and be stately, slender, soft-spoken, and willing to spend her time sewing tapestries.

Dorma's eyes were gray and nearsighted—from reading, some whispered. Her brown hair had been chopped off just above her shoulders when she got it tangled in her tiara. Though her skin was clear, she often wandered off without a parasol, so that her nose was freckled. Royalty, as everybody knew, was supposed to be immune to even a freckle.

At least Dorma was soft-spoken, so much so that nobody could make out what she was saying.

While she *was* slender, she had trouble finding a graceful way to arrange her hands and feet, and she bit her fingernails when she was ill at ease, which was often.

For ten years she had sewn a tapestry, begun when she was seven. Finally she had put it up in the throne room. The tapestry was a work of such unwholesome colors and ill-formed objects that foreign ambassadors who gazed upon it became snappish and unreasonable. Wincealot had the stitchery carted to the dungeons, where, it was rumored, prisoners pleaded for any punishment rather than being left alone with it.

Dorma had started out all wrong simply by being born. Wincealot tried to overlook her, since proper kings produced sons to inherit their thrones. As years passed, and no male heir appeared, he stopped speaking to the queen, who left Minervia one spring saying she was going on vacation. She was never heard from again. There were rumors she'd become a witch, whispers that she'd run away with a troupe of traveling troubadours. Wincealot would have banished her brother Arnold if Arnold hadn't always said she was a flibbertigibbet—and if Wincealot had had any idea how to run a kingdom himself.

Dorma was turned over to nursemaids, who had no great interest in her, and to tutors, who let her look at books in order to keep her quiet and out from underfoot. With no playmates, and no parents to speak of, or to, the princess taught herself to read, a habit hardly anyone suspected.

Other than that, she strove to be a proper princess in the hope that someday someone would approve of something about her.

She tried to get the maids to keep the palace neat, hoping her father would notice, but all the servants ignored her. So she began tidying up herself, which only reminded people of what a disgrace she was.

She set the broom in the corner, now, and trudged back up to her chambers.

The king gazed after her. "Look at her. What happened to all her hair? And she doesn't even walk like a princess. She scuffs. Can't someone teach her to look stately, at least?"

"That's what those handmaidens are supposed to do," Arnold murmured.

"They're no good," Wincealot said. "They're ashamed to be seen with her."

"You need someone who can terrify her into behaving royally."

"What about the dragon?"

"We don't need to terrify her that much," Arnold protested.

"I mean, what are we going to do about that creature that attacks my kingdom?"

"Ah. Well. It comes down to this: The beast must be eliminated."

Eyes flashing, the king forgot all about his wretched child. "A crusade! We'll round up all the knights in Minervia!"

Arnold shook his head. "Bad. Bad. Very bad.

That would only call attention to our dragon problem."

"Dragon problem." Wincealot nodded soberly. "Of course."

"Look, a dragon is an old-fashioned animal, right? In dealing with old-fashioned problems, old-fashioned ways can be best. Fight fire with fire, and all that."

"*Fire?*"

"Merely a figure of speech. What you must do is appoint a dragon slayer. Pick one knight and order him to kill the monster."

"Why me?"

"Because when you were crowned you took an oath to fulfill your responsibilities, that's why you," the high commissioner reminded him sharply.

"Since when is a dragon my responsibility?"

"Since you were crowned, that's when."

"And you know what will happen? You know what will happen? I appoint a knight to kill your dragon. A knight with any brains will refuse. Since nobody may refuse the king, I'll have to banish him. Of course, if he has no sense, he'll go and get himself killed by the beast. I appoint another knight, then another. Suppose one is finally lucky enough to slay the creature. I'll have my sensible knights off in exile, my brave knights dead, and some stupid hero parading around here expecting constant applause. *And that will be my only knight!*"

"That's what we really need, of course."

"Some stupid hero parading around?" the king asked.

"No, no. A genuine hero. Someone like the Black Knight of Doum. They say he was totally unknown when he appeared at the great tournament in Doum, defeated every man on the field, and was knighted then and there. Doum knows how to attract heroes."

"Don't start on that," Wincealot warned.

"Doum attracts heroes because it has splendid tournaments." While Arnold knew Wincealot loathed any talk of tournaments, he could not overlook the opportunity to make a point. "It has fine tournaments because it has a fine tournament field, not some run-down arena undermined by gophers and overgrown with weeds."

The king had been promising for years to have Minervia's field put in shape. Not even he was aware of the reason he let the project lag. He could not admit, even to himself, his fear that Minervia's knights were quarrelsome only among themselves; that, should Minervia ever hold a tournament, it might be profoundly humiliated.

He scowled now, to hide his discomfort. "And what did Doum get in that genuine hero? Some nobody who is dubbed the Black Knight and then goes where he pleases, does what he pleases. Besides, everybody says he's as fierce and dangerous as any dragon."

Though Arnold had never met anyone who'd

actually seen the Black Knight, he had heard tales of that notable's recklessness. Since Arnold saw no point in pursuing an argument he seemed to be losing, he said, "Let's give this dragon business more thought."

Wincealot brooded for days, with the bellowing of the new governess hired for Dorma echoing through the palace.

"Maybe we should send for a sorcerer," the king told Arnold at last.

"A *what*?"

"Sorcerer. You know—an enchanter, wizard, thaumaturge, magus, haruspex . . ."

Arnold shuddered. "Nobody in his right mind meddles with sorcerers! Give this governess a little time. She's only met the girl."

"I mean for the dragon."

"You'd be safer going up to the monster yourself! At least you know what a dragon is likely to do. Put any ideas about sorcerers out of your head. I'll go back to the village and investigate further."

"Who is Further?" asked the king.

The high commissioner was dining at the village inn that evening when a traveler entered, a thin, sunburned young man who sat at a table near the kitchen, ordered soup, and took a book from his pocket.

The high commissioner, who considered reading unwholesome, unmanly, and unnecessary, said stiffly, "In this kingdom, we have better manners than to use books in public."

The traveler opened the volume.

"We don't sit ignoring our betters who try to make polite conversation," Arnold growled.

The traveler turned a page.

Beckoning to the red-bearded innkeeper, the high commissioner said, "That man is insulting me. Throw him out."

The innkeeper clapped a great callused hand on the traveler's shoulder and suddenly found himself sitting on the floor.

Two Minervian knights who'd been hanging around the inn in the hope something might turn up—a quest, a challenge, an invitation to dinner —drew their swords, delighted by the opportunity to impress the high commissioner.

Seeing two armed knights threaten an unarmed traveler, young Hugh, a farmer's son who had been sent up to the dragon eight years earlier, kicked back his chair and leaped to his feet. But the traveler sidestepped the first knight's sword thrust, shoved him into the second, and before they could sort themselves out, tossed both their swords through the window.

Patting his beard with a napkin, Arnold stood and cleared his throat. "Why don't we talk this over, traveler? Would you do me the honor of sharing my table?"

Glancing briefly at the high commissioner, the traveler returned to his own table. Glancing at each other, the knights stood up and strolled outside to look for their swords.

Young Hugh, a tall, strongly built young man with dark gray eyes, white teeth, and thick, straight hair, hair as black as a dungeon, sat down across from the stranger.

Stepping closer to their table, Arnold spoke over Hugh's shoulder to the traveler. "How would you like to see Minervia's palace? Someone there would love to meet you."

"Thank you, no."

Hugh grinned at the stranger's coolness.

Hugh had been sent up to the dragon when he was barely twelve, by unanimous recommendation of the villagers. He had stayed with the dragon only a few months before running off. Now, eight years after being sacrificed, he had returned to Minervia with nothing to say about where he'd been, or what he'd done in the years after he'd left the dragon. He'd been home only a week, and already his father was hoping he'd leave again before he was hanged, for the lad had learned absolutely no respect for his betters.

In the days he'd been back, in fact, Hugh had made most of his family nervous. He was kind to his parents, patient with his brothers and sisters, but he was different, like a wolf who'd wandered into a dog pack. While he was amiable enough, the villagers sensed that he was no longer one of them.

He had become a solitary.

The high commissioner hiked his chair closer to the traveler now. "It's the king would like to meet you."

"I have no time for kings. I'm looking for work."

Arnold's beard quivered. "Work? Work? You're looking for work? Oh, my boy, you must come to the palace. We'll have jesters and minstrels and mead."

"Jesters and minstrels and mead." Returning, the first knight sheathed his sword. "Let me dust your boots for you, traveler."

"Dancing bears and perfumed fountains," Arnold added.

"Perfumed bears and dancing fountains," the second knight said. "'ere, let me 'ave your coat brushed for you."

The innkeeper smiled down at the stranger. "You can wash up in my kitchen, friend."

The traveler stood up.

"You're going?" Hugh asked.

The traveler shrugged. "How can I disappoint such well-wishers?"

three

UST you drag every rag-tag vagabond you bag in here?" Wincealot demanded.

"You tell me when I have ever brought a soul into this palace before," the high commissioner retorted indignantly, "and if you can't behave, I may not even tell you why I invited him."

"I don't care," Wincealot muttered. "His boots are a disgrace. Why?"

"Merely to save our kingdom. But that's all right. I'll tell him he can't deliver us because his boots are shabby."

"Save the kingdom how?" Wincelot demanded.

"We can't have just *anybody* rescuing us."

"Save it how?" The king's face took on a purplish hue.

"That young man with the disreputable boots is as fierce as an eagle, agile as an eel, supple as a serpent—a born dragon slayer. And, equally important, a stranger. If he says he'd rather be exiled than fight our dragon, tell him he can't be exiled, since he's from another place already. If he challenges the beast and is . . . if we lose him, we haven't lost anybody we know. How else could we get rid of a dragon without spending a knight?"

"What if he kills it, and hangs around expecting constant admiration?"

"Then you deport him. He doesn't belong here anyway."

Princess Dorma came tripping into the throne room.

"Oh, for heaven's sake! Watch your feet!" her father snapped.

"I'm not allowed to," she murmured. "It isn't stately."

Ignoring her, the high commissioner went out and brought the stranger back to the throne room. "Your Majesty, this is . . . what's your name?"

"Miles Bowman."

From the throne, Wincealot gazed cordially at the stranger. "So, Miles Bowman, I hear you're going to kill our dragon."

Miles went pale under his sunburn. Dorma went even paler.

Arnold rolled his eyes toward the ceiling. "Tact," he muttered. "Diplomacy."

"Ah . . . tell us something about yourself," the ruler went on hastily. "How do you stand on dragons?"

"Very carefully, I should think."

The monarch looked stern. "I hope you're not in favor of monsters ravaging the countryside, terrorizing inhabitants."

"Never," Miles said.

"Splendid. You start immediately." The king was plainly relieved at getting a bothersome chore off his hands.

"I am not going to murder a beast who's given me no first-hand reason to disturb him. I quit, now."

"Not before we show you around." Arnold pulled on a velvet rope.

A score of guards entered, wearing green tights, purple doublets, and orange hats with lavender plumes. Dorma's mother had designed the uniforms before she lost interest in being a queen.

"You really must see our dungeons," the high commissioner said. "Full of bottomless pits."

"And crocodiles," Wincealot added. "Whole families of imported crocodiles."

The stranger was calm. "They'd probably add up to one small dragon."

"You said you were looking for work," Arnold reminded him.

"Decent work."

"Right!" Dorma breathed, but nobody noticed.

35

"Excuse us a moment." The high commissioner led the king out of the throne room. "I've got an idea. He wants work, we'll give him work. We'll make him our census taker."

"You devil!" Wincealot chortled. "But how would that solve the dragon problem? It attacks our census takers when they try to count it. That's why we're always out of census takers."

"But this is not a man to flee from a mere dragon. Besides, he'd need half a mile's head start to outrun it."

Left in the throne room with the stranger, Dorma tried to tell him how she admired his principles. She got only as far as clearing her throat repeatedly.

Poor thing, Miles thought. Probably some jester's unfortunate child.

"All right." Arnold returned with the king. "We have a decent job for you—important, even. And you get a title. You'll be our census taker. How's that?"

"Don't sign anything!" Dorma cried.

For a moment, she had her father's wholehearted attention. His face flushed, he shouted, "Get her out of my sight!"

As she was led away, her uncle said, "Maybe the lessons are too much for her."

"Make her take dancing, then," the ruler snapped. "If her brain is weak, at least keep her feet occupied." Then he went on to explain the census taker's duties to Miles. "You are to count

every man, woman, child, and beast in Minervia
. . . starting with the dragon."

The traveler's eyes narrowed, and he took a long stride toward the throne. In an instant, he was ringed by guards with leveled spears.

If he had to go down fighting, he decided, better a dragon than twenty clowns in green and purple.

Seeing him hesitate, Arnold smiled. "Well. Shall we get down to business, then?"

He rented Miles a lance and a suit of armor, and permitted him to hire a palace page.

It was not yet dawn when Miles set out for the monster's lair.

"We can't have you parading around attracting attention to our dragon problem before it's solved," Arnold explained.

Miles and the page plodded through the village, harried by barking dogs, and climbed the path through the foothills, then clambered up the mountain. A hundred yards below the den, the page buckled Miles into the armor and ran.

By the time he had struggled to the mouth of the lair, the traveler felt as if he were simmering in a kettle. He peered into the cave. "This won't take a moment of your time . . ."

The dragon, interrupted in his dying, let out a *Whoosh!* of astonishment that tumbled Miles off the ledge and down the mountainside. Stunned, trapped in the scorched and dented armor, Miles saw a great hulk slither from the lair, blotting out the sun. As the monster thundered down the mountain, breathing crimson flame, the man scrambled to his knees and jammed the butt of the lance against a boulder.

The beast had never before met a human who threatened it—only fleeing Minervians and their untidy young. It lumbered right into the lance.

"*Wow! Woo! Woo Ha!*" Rearing back, it fell head over heels, heels, and heels, and crashed far below, where it lay shrieking, massive tail switching wildly.

Miles clambered down the rocks to where the creature floundered. At the sight of its suffering, tears filled his eyes, then his helmet. "Poor thing. Poor loathesome reptile. I can't let it lie here in agony."

He raised what was left of the lance.

The dragon stopped writhing and stared at him with enormous bloodshot eyes. "*What are you doing?*"

"Poor beast. I'm putting you out of your misery."

"You leave me in my misery! Go away!"

"I can't leave you in such pain."

"Who says it's fatal?" The creature peered down at its belly. "Ohhh . . . the sight of blood always did make me squeamish."

"Put your head down," Miles suggested. "Breathe deep. No! *In,* not at me."

When its giddiness had passed, the beast

twisted to stare at the wound again. "You pinked me!"

"How could I help it? First you whoosh me down the mountain, then you come slithering at me before I can stand up. That's hardly sporting."

"Who ever heard of a sporting dragon? And who was it invaded my den done up in iron? Is that how you dress for a social call?"

"You ought to tend to that nick," the traveler advised, to change an awkward subject.

"I ought to? *I* ought to? Did I come along and stab myself? With all that 'sporting' drivel, the least you could do is lend a hand."

With a formidable effort, Miles kept his patience. "All right. I'll take you down to the village and get you tended."

"That's it, is it? Parade me through the kingdom. Maybe a collar and a leash. Young man, I have lived too long to end my days in some cage." He lay back, all his legs limp, his scaly old throat bared. "Kill me. Go ahead. Kill me now, if you have any gram of decency left."

"You must be the world's most exasperating reptile," Miles snapped. "You can lie there all day, but I'm not going to kill you unless you need it. And I refuse to be seen in public with a grumbling old dragon. If you come back to your den, I'll patch that scratch and get out of your kingdom as soon as I count it."

"You're a stranger?"

The man nodded.

"Then why in the world come annoy me?"

"I'll tell you on the way. It will help pass the climb."

He did, and it did.

"*Will* you stop shuddering while I work," Miles growled.

"I can't help it. If humans ever looked at themselves, all pinkish and scurrying . . ." But he tried to stop shivering, for he'd never had a bandage before. Even though it was only the stranger's shirt, the dressing was a matter of some pride to the beast, who fancied it looked rather dashing. "You know, I resent that about my ravishing kingdoms. I've had a bit of fun in my day, but I never really lost my temper until I thought they were sending up thirty of their spawn. However, it seems to me it's you who have the problem. If you go back to the palace without killing me, it's dungeons and alligators for you. And if you're caught trying to sneak out of Minervia . . ."

"May I have something to drink?"

"Certainly." He watched the man dip water from the stream that ran through the cavern. "You could stay here a few days to think things over. My youths and maidens were a miserable lot, but it does get quiet without them. I don't suppose you play chess. I believe one of my sacrifices left a set around here somewhere."

*　*　*

While the king and court waited for news of the dragon's demise, Dorma came dancing into the throne room.

"What is she *doing,* dancing into my throne room?" demanded the ruler.

The dancing instructor let go of the princess and fled gracefully, but Dorma held her ground. "If I walked in, you'd ignore me, Father. You always do. You've been avoiding me all day—all my life, actually."

"What is she mumbling about?" the king asked Arnold.

Dorma forced herself to speak slowly and clearly. "I have been overlooked and underestimated all my life, but this dragon business is too much. If I don't protest, I will never respect myself. You had no right to trick that man, and no right to harass the dragon. It was here before any of us. With people moving up the mountain and building right under its whiskers, do you wonder the creature gets crochety?"

Wincealot's indignation quite overcame his astonishment. *"Remove her!"*

". . . if you'd ever taken the trouble to learn the first thing about dragons . . ."

As she was hauled away by his guards, a ghastly suspicion struck the monarch. Could there be some truth in the rumors about her reading secretly?

Putting the thought out of his mind, the king

trudged up to the battlements, where, brooding, surrounded by his court, he waited for dragon news.

He hardly noticed the gasps and whispers until Arnold gripped his arm. Lords and ladies clustered at the battlements, staring at something below, whispering and nudging one another. Shoving them aside, Wincealot looked down.

His daughter, his only child, was pacing far below, carrying a cloth stretched between sticks and held so the printing on it could be read by everyone above:

UNFAIR TO STRANGERS!
SAVE THE DRAGON!
VOTES FOR MINERVIANS!!

"Dorma!" he shouted. "Go to your chambers!"

She went on pacing.

"Come up here!" he roared.

Finally, he turned to the high commissioner. "Do something!"

Arnold went down and talked to her while she picketed. At last he came back. "She says we were beastly to the man and inhuman to the beast. She wants us to rescue the stranger and come to an understanding with the dragon. She also demands votes for the people."

"What are votes?" Wincealot asked.

"I don't know. If they don't cost much, maybe you should buy some to keep her quiet."

"Buy her nothing! She'll be sent to her—"

"She's attracting quite a bit of attention," Arnold murmured. "I would advise negotiation."

"All right," the king said distractedly. "Tell her she may have a negotiation."

He went down to the throne room and looked as regal as he could when Arnold brought her in.

"Now, Dorma, what is all this nonsense?" Wincealot demanded.

Her father had never called her by name before. Dorma was so touched that tears came to her eyes, but she knew that if she backed down now she might never get the courage to stand up to anybody again.

"Answer me!" he commanded.

She did. She made herself look straight at him and tell him everything she'd been rehearsing under her breath while picketing. She insisted that the stranger be rescued at once, and that the dragon be approached reasonably. Then she added a suggestion she'd been thinking about for a long time. "You should also give every citizen of Minervia a vote."

"What is a vote?" the king asked.

She explained.

He called for his guards, who hauled the princess to her chambers and locked her in.

Even three floors below, he could hear her pounding on her door. *"You invited me in for negotiation!"*

Wearily, the king turned to his high commissioner. "What," he asked, "is a negotiation?"

four

HILE they played chess on the ledge outside the lair, the dragon sunned his scales and admired his bandage. It was afternoon when, glancing over the edge, he suddenly cried, "Oh, no!" and collapsed on his side. With a trembling claw, he pointed.

Far below, tangled hair gleaming in the sun, was—

"A maiden!" groaned the reptile. "And just when we were getting on so well. There'll be nine more. There always have been. And ten youths. They'll drive you away. I know they will. Nobody but a beast would put up with them. Oh, I am so furious I could go root up their nests! I would! But my wound . . ." He coughed delicately. "You'll have to deal with them. Wear your armor, though. You must intimidate them."

Calming the brute, Miles clambered, clanking, down the cliff.

The maiden was struggling uphill, carrying a large, leaky hamper. Muddy, panting, she put it down and smiled when she saw him. "You're alive!" Then her lovely, nearsighted gray eyes clouded. "You didn't kill the dragon?"

He couldn't imagine why people let her wander like this, soaking wet, her arms and hands scraped, dress torn. He would be firm with her. Kind, but firm. "The dragon is under control, and you must go straight home."

"I knew it!" She wiped her brow with a tattered sleeve. "I could see you were a person who understood dragons. Something about your eyes. I've come as a protest, and to start negotiations. If you'll help carry my hamper to the lair . . ."

"You can't go up there."

"I can't go back. My father will have me locked in a room with no windows this time."

Miles was hot and bruised and tired of Minervians. Putting the hamper in the princess's arms, he turned her firmly around. "Go directly home. Promise your father to stop roaming, and I'm sure he'll find you a hut with a window."

Before she could argue, he turned and climbed back to the den.

The dragon was crouched at the rear of the cavern.

"No problem," Miles said. "Nothing to worry about."

"She's gone?"

From the mouth of the cave came a soft but determined voice. "I've come—"

"No! No sacrifices!" The creature threw up all his claws. "I've been wounded."

"*Wounded*? Oh, I was afraid something like that would happen." Dorma felt her knees going wavy, but she hurried into the cave, sat on the rocky floor, and began pulling things out of the hamper. "I brought . . . scrolls . . . to write on. I wrapped everything carefully, but they did get wet. Pot of ink. Reed pens."

The dragon rolled a nervous eye, and Miles stood up. "Time to go."

"Yes, yes, time to go." The beast waved a claw airily. "So good of you to drop by."

Desperately, Dorma began dragging things out of the hamper. "Tea. Cakes . . . soggy. Here! Bandages."

Miles took her arm.

"Wait," the dragon said. "She brought bandages."

"She's also bound to bring trouble."

"Lovely, rolled up, clean bandages." The beast eyed the basket. "And yummies."

"Keep the hamper and send her back, then."

"Dragon," Dorma addressed the beast. She could see that he was going to be more reasonable than the man. "Do you have a name?"

"The hermit who shared my cave when I was no bigger than a basilisk called me Blystfylyl —or else he had a bit of beard caught in his teeth."

46

"Hermit," she murmured. "That explains how well you speak."

"There've been hermits, recluses, outcasts crawling in here for centuries. And you can't have humans around without picking up *something* from them. Dragons are a highly intelligent life form, you know, and with a forked tongue and yards of vocal cords, I'd be a dolt if I couldn't talk any better than my sacrifices."

"So, Bl . . . Bl . . . may I call you Blys? Blys, the first thing we must do is make up a list of demands."

"The first thing," the beast said, "is to have a spot of tea and cakes."

"No. That comes later. Once my father suspects where I've gone, he'll be sending troops to rescue me, so I have to be able to head them off and tell them you've agreed—"

"Troops?" The dragon paled to a cucumber shade. "Who is your father?"

"King Wincealot."

"Merciful fangs!"

"Don't be ridiculous. Look at her," Miles reassured the reptile. "All wet and dirty and unkempt . . ."

"You expect me to climb down a castle wall and swim a moat and not show it?" the maiden asked.

"Swim the moat?" Miles smiled. "With a hamper?"

"That's how everything got wet. Now, first, the demands."

The dragon's tail was twitching alarmingly. Miles stood up.

She stood up, too, and the look in her eye made him suspect that removing her might not be easy.

He was right. She struggled furiously, raging and hammering on his armor, all the way to the foothills.

When he set her down, she stood glaring at him. "Hauling people down a mountain is hardly a substitute for negotiation."

"Varlet! Knave! Unhand that maiden!" A tall, strapping youth, with storm-gray eyes and hair as black as a sorcerer's art, leaped over a boulder to face the traveler.

"You!" Miles was astonished to see Hugh, the farmer's son who had befriended him at the inn.

"You!" Hugh's voice was as cold as a dungeon floor. "I heard a rumor that you'd come to kill the dragon. I hurried here to interfere, only to find you alive and persecuting this poor drenched wretched wench."

"Do go away," Dorma told the farmer's son.

Exasperated almost beyond endurance, Miles turned back toward the cave.

As Hugh lunged after him, Dorma caught her protector's sleeve. "*Will* you stay out of this!"

"Yes, yes. I'll see you safely home after I settle with the knave who abused you." Pulling free of her, he strode after Miles.

Dorma ran after them.

"Varlet!" Catching up with Miles, Hugh swung him around, but Dorma, close behind, seized Hugh's arm, lost her balance on the steep slope, and fell, pulling her rescuer down with her. Before Hugh could scramble to his feet, Miles was on him, the remains of the rented lance at Hugh's throat.

"Don't you dare hurt him!" Dorma panted. "He's only a muddled oaf."

After being attacked by innkeepers and knights, tricked by kings and high commissioners, whooshed off a ledge by a dragon, belabored by a maiden, and reviled by Hugh, Miles had no scrap of patience left. "Then tie him," he rasped. "If you don't want to see him damaged, tie him."

It seemed to Dorma a sensible suggestion, and the most likely way to keep her hotheaded protector out of trouble. While Miles held the lance to Hugh's throat, she took the laces from Hugh's boots and bound his arms and legs.

"Now, maiden, you go home," Miles' voice was hard.

"But what about him?" She gazed down at Hugh.

"He's your problem. Roll him down to the village—I don't care." Turning, Miles started back to the lair, leaving Dorma with her fettered rescuer.

"Untie me, maiden," Hugh demanded.

"I just finished tying you," she pointed out.

"You can't leave me lying here."

"But I did such a good job."

"You'd leave a defenseless man lying helpless against scorpions and serpent stings?"

"Will you behave sensibly if I free you?"

"Naturally."

"Swear it."

"I swear."

Dorma took Hugh's sword from its scabbard. "Hold still." With one swift stroke she sliced his bootlaces, not even nicking his ankles.

"Now *untie* my hands."

"I don't think so. There's something about your eyes. You'd be better off walking home with your hands tied."

"At least help me up."

Putting down the sword, she did.

He bent to seize the weapon in bound hands, then lumbered toward the den. "No man leaves me trussed like a turkey in the middle of a mountain."

"You swore to be sensible!"

"Exactly. It makes no sense to let that varlet mistreat a maiden and then make a fool of me."

She scrambled after him, but he was a strapping, powerful man filled with rage and shame, and she had already descended a palace wall, swum a moat, and climbed the mountain. By the time she caught up with him, he had reached the ledge outside the lair and was shouting his third "Varlet!"

Blys threw up all his claws. "That does it!" Before Miles could stop him, the beast thundered out of the den. *"No sacrifices!"* Then, seeing Hugh, he reared back on his tail. *"You!"*

"You!" snapped the farmer's son. "Have you gone soft in the skull? Up here socializing with the slayer sent to do you in! What kind of beast have you become? And what kind of hero is he?"

Miles stepped out of the cave. The set of his jaw would have given a crocodile pause, but Hugh was too indignant to notice.

"Get rid of him!" the dragon begged the traveler. "I had him on my claws for months!"

Miles stepped toward Hugh.

"He called you a fraud, stranger," Dorma panted. "And you a soft-headed dragon, Blys."

"Make them go away," the beast implored Miles.

"If the kingdom is upset by a dragon, how will it react to a soft-headed dragon?" Dorma sat on a rock to catch her breath. "Think of the shame. Think of the ridicule. Think of the disgrace."

"Let me think," Miles interrupted.

"Would Minervia hesitate to attack the dragon if they thought he was a humbug? Would they withhold you from the crocodiles if they thought you were a fraud? What you and Blys must do is negotiate with what's-his-name here."

"Hugh," the farmer's son said.

By now, the beast had noticed Hugh's bound hands. "I would rather terrorize him than negotiate."

"What kind of beast would terrorize a man

whose wrists are tied?'' the princess demanded.

"My kind.'' The monster bared his fangs.

"Untie me, then,'' Hugh told Dorma.

"I can't. I'm all unstrung.''

"Somebody has to,'' he insisted, "before I go permanently numb.''

"If I do,'' she asked, "will you promise to sit quietly and listen and not challenge anybody?''

"Promise.''

"No tricks.''

"None.''

As she started to untie Hugh, the beast began flexing his claws ominously.

"No, she's right,'' Miles assured the old reptile. "We can't have either of them going back to tell people I'm alive and you're . . . ah . . . somewhat overrated. Bring him into the den, wench.''

"I will not have him back!'' Blys protested. "He's not even tame!''

"Would you prefer armies?'' Miles asked.

The creature retreated, muttering, to the dark recesses of his cavern, and Miles took off his armor while Dorma explained to Hugh about justice and ethics and the absurdity of people killing everything that inconvenienced them. "There are few enough dragons left in the world,'' she added.

"Of course, you don't think about that when one is trampling your village,'' the farmer's son observed.

"I've worked out a plan for saving the village and Minervia and the dragon and the stranger and even you.''

When she'd finished explaining it, Miles said, "It does make sense."

"It's brilliant," Hugh said. "Maiden, you are not only brave and lovely, you're the most intelligent person I've ever met. The moment I see you safely home, I shall ask permission to court you."

"Hugh," she said patiently, "first things first. The first thing is how we're going to save Miles and—"

"Miles." He leveled a long, cold look at the traveler. "Everything is Miles, Miles, Miles. When I heard you were going to kill the dragon, I hurried after you. Did I complain because you were still alive? If the woman I love wants you, I might even give you a fair chance. But I will never forgive your making a simpering, tulip-livered ninny out of our only dragon."

"Tut!" Blys handed Miles the splintered lance. "Here we go."

"Oh, nonsense," Dorma said.

"Outside," Miles told Hugh.

"Not now!" But as the princess stood to intercept the men, the beast blocked her way.

"If you don't make them stop, Blys," she threatened, "your conscience will torment you to the end of your days."

"Dragons don't have consciences."

"Then I will torment you. I'll send up sacrifices, youths and maidens."

He cringed. "People expect too much of dragons. They always have."

"I will bring up dozens of my twittering handmaidens."

He slithered to the mouth of his lair. "STOP THAT NONSENSE OUT THERE!"

He had always been careful not to roar near his cave, and for good reason.

Far up the mountain there was a rumbling, like the echo of his bellow. It grew in an instant to a thundering, deafening bombilation. Before he could move, he and the princess were sealed inside his den by tons of fallen shale.

Choking, blinded by dust, Dorma heard the old monster's wail. *"See what you made me do?"*

"What . . ." she gasped.

"An alavanche."

"Avalanche?" Scrambling to the cave's mouth, she began clawing at the rock.

Even with the dragon's help, it was no use.

"If I could get up enough steam," the beast wheezed finally, "I might breathe enough flame to melt the rocks. But you know what we'd be in then?"

She nodded. "Lava."

ﬁve

S soon as he had stepped outside the cave, Miles lowered the lance. "Look, this happens to be a very sensitive dragon. We'll go back in, and you apologize to him, and then we can sit down and negotiate."

It was then that the beast roared.

There was a booming, a convulsion as if all the world's skies had burst at once, and in a second the two men were tumbled down the mountain in a torrent of stone.

Landing in a jumble of rocks, Miles lay still a moment. From the way he hurt, he felt sure he was still alive. As he struggled free of the rubble, he saw, a little way to his left, a boot with no laces. He tore at the rocks around it until he unearthed Hugh.

The farmer's son sat up, dazed. "What happened?"

Miles looked toward where the dragon's den had been. "Uh . . . the top of the mountain is now all over the mountain."

"The maiden!" Scrambling to his feet, Hugh clambered over loose shale and uprooted trees, Miles behind him. Desperately, they searched for the den.

Finally, exhausted, despairing, Miles leaned against a boulder. "We may never . . . Wait! This rock . . . it's warmer than the others!"

Hugh put a hand against it. "Dragon breath! It must be heated by dragon breath from the other side!"

They shoved at the boulder until their shoulders were raw and their hands bleeding, without moving it an inch.

"We need help," Miles panted. "I'll go to the palace. You get the villagers."

"Dig out the dragon?" demanded the villagers. "Dig out the *dragon*?"

"Just go up to its den and dig it out?"

"One question. Once it's dug out . . . *wot then*?"

The villagers agreed it was a pity about the maiden. Even if she meddled with things that were none of her business, such as dragons, she hardly deserved to be sealed up with one.

"Must've been a bit dotty, trampin' up to a dragon den alone, one small maiden. Barely a snack for the beastie, which is no doubt gettin' 'ungrier and angrier the longer it's penned up."

Finally Hugh borrowed a pickax from his father and stumbled back alone toward the mountain.

"Dig out the dragon?" demanded the high commissioner.

This was some time after Miles got to the castle.

When he first reached the moat, he had been challenged by tower guards, who weren't about to admit just any dirty wild-eyed stranger with ruined boots.

"She's trapped!" he shouted. "A maiden, with the dragon. We have to dig them out."

The guards eyed his ragged clothes and bleeding hands. Then they sent three knights down to arrest him.

A bit later the high commissioner was strolling through the dungeons, on his way to visit the crocodiles, when he heard Miles ranting. "Stranger!" Arnold cried. "I've been worried sick! Where's my armor?"

"Sealed in a cave with the dragon."

"You've trapped the dragon? Marvelous! Fantastic!"

". . . and that maiden."

"Maiden?"

"The one who was in the throne room when you signed me up as census taker."

"Idiot! Knave! You'll pay for this with your life."

"We must dig them out!" Miles urged.

The high commissioner had Miles released and brought to the throne room.

"I don't want to hear another word about how he lost your armor," Wincealot warned Arnold at last. "I want to know whether he's killed our dragon. And if not, how dare he come into our presence all grubby?"

"Tell him." The high commissioner nudged Miles.

"The dragon is sealed in its den."

"You've trapped it? Fabulous! Glorious!" beamed the king.

". . . with your daughter," Arnold added.

"Daughter?" Miles was stunned. "She really is . . ."

The king shook. He howled like a wolf. He hurled hideous threats, and his crown, and his scepter.

"Really!" The high commissioner loathed scenes. "You never liked her all that much."

Tears left matted tracks down the monarch's beard. "You've never had a grown child."

"We must dig them out!" Miles said again.

The ruler's cry brought the whole court running. *Dig them out!*

"And lock up this stranger until I recover my armor," Arnold added.

In the first cold light of dawn, the knights assembled, bronze and steel moving with a sullen, lurking gleam, pennants waving over the heads of scurrying pages. Artists, summoned by the high commissioner, were hastily packing brushes and easels. Horses reared, their hooves striking sparks from the gray stones of the courtyard. Then, piercing the crowd to the heart, came the thin, sweet call of the trumpets.

The king surveyed his troops, who were jostling one another and arguing about who had the right to ride at the head of the procession. "I don't know. It might be wiser to hire a sorcerer. There's one who lives beyond . . ."

Arnold shuddered. "Have you ever met a sorcerer?"

"Have you?"

"With any luck, I never will. It's not even safe to think about sorcerers."

The Royal High Commissioner's First Annual Rescue Crusade and Outing—it should not be necessary to say who named it—arrived at the dragon mountain in a tumult of drums, trumpets, and quarreling over who had the right to ride at the end of the line.

Fifty villagers who had been forcefully persuaded to join the crusade were put to work beside Hugh, who was already struggling to move a boulder.

Arnold directed twenty archers to a spot some distance above the boulder, twenty to the left of it, twenty to the right. After arranging the knights artistically, he addressed the crusade:

"Men! The dragon, being trapped in there with himself all this time, will naturally rush out the moment the cave is opened. When you see him, archers, riddle him with arrows! Then, knights, finish him off! Finally, artists, you will paint my portrait as I stand on the carcass. This is a great day for Minervia!"

Cheering, the knights threw their helmets into the air. There was a flashing of bronze and steel, a clanging and a bounding of dented helmets, a fierce squabbling over who had picked up whose headgear.

Meanwhile, the villagers were asking one another, "Wot did 'e say?"

"What did you say?" Hugh asked the high commissioner.

"Dig them out!" Arnold commanded.

The villagers, with Hugh, gave an enormous heave on all the picks and sticks and shovels wedged around the boulder. Slowly, it rolled away from the cave mouth.

As a current of warm air wafted from the den, the villagers dropped their tools and ran. Hugh, exhausted, leaned on a pick.

"On the other hand," Arnold said, "it's never too late to call in a sorcerer."

"Aim!" called the king.

The archers drew their bows, the knights their swords.

"*Aim?*" Hugh demanded, stunned. "Are you standing there planning to betray a beast who thinks you've saved it? Has it never occurred to you that it might be grateful?"

Ragged and grimy, Dorma stumbled from the cave.

The king ran to catch her in his arms.

"It's an ambush, maiden," Hugh warned her.

"*Ambush?*" She drew back. She knew her father had never approved of her, but . . .

"Hush, my dear." The king patted her gingerly. "This is business."

Too exhausted to think of anything more eloquent, Hugh rasped, "Has it never occurred to anybody that the beast might be grateful?"

Relieved, but alarmed for the dragon, Dorma cried, "Oh, he will be! He will! I know it. He's had a sad life. Terrible childhood. He was an egg, you know."

Deep within the lair there was a slithering.

"Steady!" Wincealot called to the troops.

In a clear, ringing voice, the princess called out, "What? My father ambush the poor grateful beast who kept the cave warm and my courage up? Would my own father let himself be known through centuries to come as King Wincealot the Wretched, who shamefully slayed . . . slew . . . sloy . . . slaughtered the simple serpent who sheltered his only child?"

There was a look in her eye that made her father think of placards and picketing. And he knew, now, that she could write, or at least print. He looked around him. "Put down those stupid weapons," he told his troops.

Before they could obey, there was a rumbling inside the cave, and the earth trembled.

"Here it comes," Hugh said.

And there it came.

Four tons of ancient fury thundered from the lair behind a wall of flame.

Being buried alive does nothing for a dragon's disposition, which is prickly at best. Thinking he might be sealed up for centuries had thrown him into a depression. The steady *nik, nik, nik* of the rescuers' implements had shredded his nerves. Now, seeing scores of armed humans on his very doorstep, he lost every remnant of composure.

That dragon rush, in the winter of his time, aeons after his prime, became the stuff of epics for generations to come in kingdoms reaching to the very fringes of the world.

Even though nobody saw the whole thing.

At the first strong rumble, the horses threw their riders and galloped after the villagers. As flame whooshed from the cave, the archers let fly a few wild arrows, then scrambled after the horses, and a moment later the knights scattered.

Arnold, from behind a rock, cried, "No retreat!"

Hugh threw himself on Dorma to shield her from the stampeding crusaders, and Wincealot dove behind him.

The raging reptile lumbered down the mountain, over the ruins of the houses he'd smashed on his last rampage. Storming through the village, he trampled the inn and tore up the fields; then, charging on to the castle itself, he seared the moat, ate the drawbridge, toppled the parapets, and ruined the ramparts.

He overdid, of course.

Wheezing back to the lair, he could barely keep up appearances.

After the beast passed in that wonderful wild rush, Hugh helped the princess to her feet. How long, Dorma wondered dazedly, was she doomed to be protected by this overwhelmingly impulsive rescuer?

The king stood up, and his voice was as cold and hard as the gaze he fastened on Hugh. "You said a *grateful* dragon."

"I'd say we should be far from its den before it returns," the princess interrupted hastily.

They'd reached the very instep of the foothills when they heard breathing, as loud and discordant as the royal orchestra. Then they saw the dragon barely dragging himself along, a little faster than a horse at full gallop.

Wincealot looked around. There was not a knight or archer in sight. Nothing to hide behind. Realizing that running would only inflame the monster's killer instinct, he drew himself up, behind Hugh.

Seeing them, the beast changed course to intercept them, tongue lolling as long and red as the throne room carpet. "You have no idea what that took out of me," he panted.

"I suppose you're quite pleased with yourself," Hugh said coldly.

A ridge of scales rose along the monster's

spine. "What did you expect, gratitude? You might at least offer to pick some of these sticks out of me."

"Arrows."

"They must be streaming gore. I feel like a dart board—I daren't look."

"I suppose you expect me to see you back to your lair."

The beast looked more cheerful. "Well, you wouldn't want to go down to the village. It's a mess. And who's this, all dressed up and lurking behind you?"

"The king," Hugh said.

"Ah. Then she *is* his daughter." Blys nodded curtly at the monarch. "Do keep a closer eye on your child." Then he slithered on up the hillside, Hugh following.

"Come out of that ditch," Wincealot ordered his high commissioner. "Did you see that? Gaining its confidence so he can dispatch it unawares. *There* is a dragon slayer. Look at that bearing, that nobility. Who is that splendid young man?"

"I've seen him somewhere before." Arnold gazed after Hugh. "Royalty, obviously. Probably on a quest."

Dorma was silent. If her uncle and the king realized Hugh was a Minervian, a former sacrifice who had no interest in destroying the beast, they'd not only think Hugh a traitor, they might lose the respect for the dragon that they'd acquired so painfully.

Meanwhile, she had to consider who was

most likely to make trouble next. So she made her way, with her relatives, to the castle.

On his own territory, devastated as it was, Wincealot began to feel more forceful. His immediate concern was the noble young hero who was even now with the dragon. It was too risky to chance that splendid lad's being able to slay the beast alone. He had to be rescued quickly—and quietly. Should the beast become alarmed, it might destroy the prince in a flash. The lad's father would undoubtedly blame Minervia if he learned his son had been done in by a dragon Minervia was unable to control.

Seeing her father deep in thought, Dorma went to her chambers and began to draw up, from memory, the same peace proposal she'd presented to the dragon. After many hours she closed her eyes, to rest them a moment.

Meanwhile, the king had his scattered troops rounded up and made them draft every able-bodied man they could catch. While his daughter slept, he explained to the multitude assembled in the courtyard that this would be a stealthy, secret crusade.

His troops prepared for the mission.

Whippets and greyhounds raced, yapping, among the trumpeters and well-wishers and sellers of charms and amulets. Knights shoved and jostled, arguing in whispers over who got to ride under the pennants.

The able-bodied draftees muttered among themselves.

"Did 'e say we was goin' on a charade, Ollie?"

"I don't know, 'arry, but 'e said we'd be filthy."

A page sneered up at them. "That's *stealthy*, you crowns."

A knight sneered down at him. "That's *clowns*, you oat."

The high commissioner watched the flower of Minervian manhood prepare for the great endeavor.

"In my opinion," he told the king, "it is time to call in a sorcerer."

"Stop twitching." Hugh drew another shaft from the beast's armored hide. "I have no sympathy for you."

"If you were stuck all over with arrows, I suppose you wouldn't quiver? I feel like a porpentine."

"There'll be more of it."

"What do you *mean*?"

"They came right to your doorstep this time, didn't they? You don't think they'll let it go at that? They'll be back. Humans are like that. Once they've tried something new, they can never let it alone."

The reptile fell back in shock, all his legs waving feebly. "Spare me! They came in hordes! Hordes of nasty, arrow-throwing pink beasties." A shiver passed the length of his spine, giving

Hugh time to examine the things Dorma had brought up in the hamper. "If they come back, I will trample all their nests flat. I will! Every one of them."

"That would only excite them. They'll keep coming and coming."

The creature moaned. "I'm too old to be so abused. This is my mountain. I was here before any of them were hatched."

Hugh tossed him one of the cakes Dorma had brought. "So you wrecked the village."

He brightened. "Oh, I did. Totally. And you should see the castle!"

"It's nonsense, Blys, the whole business. They upset you, you attack them, and what do you get but a little fling that leaves you miserable? It's time to stop the whole stupid game."

six

ID we think of everything?" Hugh asked.

"Everything the princess mentioned."

"Princess. Would you have believed it? The most glorious woman I've ever met, and she turns out to be royalty. Well . . . nobody's perfect. Sign it."

"Sign what?"

"Your name. On the treaty."

"Sign?"

"A simple *B* will do." Hugh guided the great claws. "Good. Now I'll take both copies down to the king. As soon as he signs them and one is returned to you, you're at peace with Minervia."

"You think this will work?"

"It has to. Do you know how long we've spent on it?"

"It's not easy to negotiate with a dragon."

*   *   *

The secret rescue troop had been assembled for hours.

In the courtyard, those knights who were not still arguing over who had whose helmet sat listening to the latest ballads about the Black Knight of Doum.

Although no one had heard of the Knight before he appeared at the great tournament in Doum only four years earlier, that tale was well known by now: Armored all in rusty black, the anonymous challenger had defeated every man on the lists, and had refused to lift his visor or speak his name. The Prince of Doum, who was not about to have a mere nobody win his great tournament, had dubbed the victor, on the spot, the Black Knight of Doum.

In the years that followed, every wandering bard and traveling troubadour had turned up with a new ballad celebrating the hero who vanquished giants and gryphons and three-headed serpents, the hero who never showed his face.

The young knights in Minervia had taken to swaggering about with the visors of their helmets down, half smothering themselves. Though they touched up their horses with lamp-black, they were not so reckless as to affect black armor, or even so much as a black cloak. Should one ever come upon this Black Knight, there was no sense in being dressed in such a way as to offend him.

With their own tournament field a disaster, they dreamed of traveling to Doum and winning the great tournament—and they woke trembling from nightmares in which a tall, silent figure on a sable stallion loomed out of the dark on some deserted lane.

Having seen no adventure and little hope of fame for years, all the Minervian knights had been thrilled by the chance to take part in the Royal High Commissioner's First Annual Rescue Crusade and Outing.

After seeing the dragon, however, they had become thoughtful and subdued. Summoned to a second crusade so soon after the first, they sat listening to ballads about the Black Knight's battles and staring at the cold stone of the courtyard.

They had met the dragon.

They knew, now, that the way to Doum was long and probably uncomfortable, and that dragons do not always lose.

Nobody noticed Hugh as he made his way out of the rubble-filled moat and strode across the courtyard.

Nobody but the guard at the palace portals heard him say, "Inform the king that I'm back from the dragon."

" 'oo is?" the guard demanded.

"Hugh is."

"Me? I never went near no dragon!"

Arnold, who was pacing the great hall, waiting for a reply from the sorcerer, heard the word "dragon," peered toward the portals, and saw the farmer's son. "You're back! Alive!" Sending a page to announce the news, he ushered Hugh into the council chambers. "Look! Back! Alive!"

Wincealot hurried to them and grasped Hugh's hand, too relieved to speak.

Nobles and councillors crowded into the chambers to see the foreign prince who'd gone up to the dragon's and come back alive. Pages and servants scurried through the palace with the news.

Dorma had protested against the secret crusade so vehemently that her father had had her shut up in her chambers with a dozen of her handmaidens, who had strict orders not to allow her out. Now, hearing of the prince who'd come back after conquering the dragon, the handmaidens rushed to their rooms to freshen up before dashing down to see the royal hero.

In the council chambers, Hugh unrolled the scrolls on the long table. "We've got an agreement with the beast. A treaty. Once you've signed, we'll be at peace with him."

"Just tell me what it says," Wincealot murmured. "Don't make me read it."

Arnold was scandalized. "A treaty? With a dragon? Who ever heard of negotiating with a reptile?"

"The dragon will stay on his mountain if you promise, first, never to send up another youth or maiden," Hugh said.

Arnold peered at the scrolls. "Demands from a dragon?"

". . . or to permit anyone to set foot on his territory without his consent," Hugh went on.

Dorma hurried into the council chambers. "Hugh, did you?"

He nodded.

"You did it!" she chortled.

After Hugh explained the rest of the treaty, the king said, "Why didn't anyone think of this before?"

"Sign both copies where it says *for Minervia*," Hugh told him, "date them, then you keep one and have the other delivered to the dragon."

"Nobody makes treaties with reptiles," the high commissioner bristled.

"It's a good agreement," the ruler insisted.

Drawing Wincealot toward the door, Arnold said, "The king and I must confer privately."

Outside the chambers, he hissed, "Don't sign anything! The sorcerer should be here any time now."

"You said yourself a dragon was safer than a sorcerer."

"That was before I saw the dragon."

"Oh, come on, Arnold. It's a fine treaty, and a way to settle the dragon business right now, and my daughter would have a fit if she knew you sent for a sorcerer."

"Have I ever given you bad advice?"

"You told me to appoint a dragon slayer. You told me to make that traveler a census taker. When he got the princess sealed in a cave with the dragon, you told me to organize the rescue crusade, which ended up with the beast squashing half of Minervia. You told me not to think of a sorcerer, then you sent for a sorcerer."

"Well, if you're going to dig up every little thing . . ."

"Besides, we can't insult that young man who brought the treaty. You said yourself he must be royalty."

"And do you think he'd have the slightest respect for a kingdom that is too soft to do away with its own dragon?"

"But he recommends the agreement . . . and he seems fond of my daughter."

"That's all right. Give him an honor or something, then wait for the sorcerer. Do you think a prince of that stature would marry into a family that would buckle under to demands from a dragon?"

When they returned to the council chambers, Wincealot said to Hugh, "First, for your extraordinary bravery and devotion to our welfare, we should like to make you an honorary lord of the realm, if you don't object."

"I suppose not," Hugh said. "But now for the treaty—"

"You're sure your father won't mind?" the king asked.

"He won't care one way or the other."

Wincealot tapped him on the shoulder with a sword. "We hereby dub thee a lord of the realm of Minervia. Now for the treaty. We've decided not to sign it."

"Not sign?" Hugh's eyes darkened and he took a step forward. "You expect me to go back to my village and say you refuse to make peace with the dragon?"

The king was bewildered. "Your what?"

"My village. Right in the path of every dragon raid. Smashed, trampled, along with my poor father's farm."

Wincealot's bellow made knights and nobles tremble. "Fraud! Cheat! Imposter! How dared you pretend to be royalty? *Guards!*"

"I'm afraid Hugh will have to be going," Dorma said quickly. "The dragon is so . . . interested in his welfare. We wouldn't want it to come looking for him if it learned he was in difficulty."

Knights and nobles gasped, aghast.

The king looked for a long moment at his daughter. She had, after all, managed to visit the beast once before. "Go back to sleep," he told the guards who'd come running. "I only wanted to see if you were paying attention." He glared at Arnold. "Real royalty, you said."

"*You* said."

"Don't you say another word!" Snatching a pen from the inkstand, Wincealot scrawled his name on both copies of the treaty and handed one to Arnold. "Deliver it."

The high commissioner looked at the treaty as if it were spitting venom. "Me? I don't know anything about dragons."

"Until now, you've known everything about everything."

Arnold turned to Hugh. "If anyone deserves the honor, it's you."

The king's voice made the councillors edge closer together. "You would send up a treaty in the hands of a peasant?"

"There must be someone here willing to take it to the dragon." Arnold looked around the chamber.

The nobles began murmuring about how wonderful treaties were and how desperately they regretted having weak hearts and nervous stomachs.

Disgusted, Hugh said, "Give it to me."

"You." Wincealot turned on him. "You should consider yourself lucky to be merely banished. Leave our presence at once and our kingdom by the quickest route!"

Dorma followed Hugh from the palace.

In the courtyard, a few knights were trying to sleep, armor clanking as they shifted. Peddlers were setting up tents, vendors were roasting potatoes, while fortune-tellers in tattered finery laid out cards.

At the moat, Hugh stopped. "Banished."

"Banished," Dorma said, "is the safest place I can think of for you right now. You tend to get yourself into situations."

"I will not stay banished. I'll come back, you know. And when I do . . ."

"Hugh, dear Hugh. You escaped the dungeon only moments ago. Will you ever learn?"

He turned away without another word.

She watched him clamber into the moat and out the other side. When he was out of sight, she walked back to the palace and went up to her chambers to work out a way to get the treaty delivered.

seven

LYS heard no sound, but something drew his gaze to the mouth of the den.

The being who stood there was tall and pale, with cold green eyes and a hood of what looked like fine green scales.

When they send someone to deliver a treaty, they send *someone!* the beast thought, impressed. At the same time, he felt a profound uneasiness.

There was a flash of light, and then a blackness even dragon eyes couldn't fathom.

"There has to be someone in Minervia brave or reckless enough to deliver the treaty," Wincealot insisted, pacing his private study.

"But how would it look," Arnold asked, "sending your own daughter?"

"We could let the stranger out of the dungeon on condition he deliver it," Wincealot suggested.

"Interesting idea," Arnold murmured. "It was the stranger who sealed the beast up in its cave."

"Mmm. But the main thing is, we have a treaty, and it didn't cost us a knight. We didn't even have to use a sorcerer. . . . *Sorcerer!*"

Arnold made a small noise, something between a whimper and a squeak.

Frantically, Wincealot pulled on a velvet rope. Nobody came.

The king rushed from his study, followed by the high commissioner. "Quick! Somebody call off the sorcerer!"

"I'm not sure you can call off a sorcerer." Arnold's voice was as small and dry as a shriveled cocoon.

They hurried through the palace without seeing a soul. Shoving open the great carved portals, they emerged into a deserted courtyard, where only potato skins, smoking embers, and a broken sandal greeted them.

Then, in the shadow of a dragon-shattered wall, something moved.

I do not see what I think I see, the king told himself.

The hooves, the body, were those of an enormous goat, the head that of a lion. The tail was the horror, the atrocity. The tail, writhing, hissing with a life of its own, was a serpent.

Chimera! the king thought, shuddering before that fabled beast.

Ghastly as the chimera was, its rider seized and held the monarch's gaze.

The rider was tall, robed in a shiny green fur, his pale, almost noble face framed in green mail like the hood of a cobra. The pupils of his glittering cold green eyes flickered and changed size and shape like black flame.

With an effort, Wincealot managed to look away from those eyes, but he could not escape the voice, as deep and cold as a winter grave. "The sorcerer is here." Effortlessly, the man dismounted. "I am Volotor. You sent for me."

"Oh, I'm . . . I'm terribly sorry, old man," the ruler quavered. "We had this dragon problem, but it's been taken care of."

"I know."

"Oh." Wincealot's voice was fading rapidly. "We . . . ah . . . we were about to send someone up there with a treaty. I hope you didn't leave the monster too upset."

"I didn't leave it. Filene . . ."

From the shadow of the wall stepped a lady dressed all in gray. Her hair was black and glossy, drawn back from a pale oval face, her eyes green and lustrous. She carried a bird cage with a large green parrot huddled on its floor.

Neither Wincealot nor Arnold could take their eyes off the cage.

The sorcerer smiled. "A bird is only a feathered reptile, after all. Don't you want it?"

The king and the high commissioner recoiled.

"You have a pet, then, Filene," the sorcerer told the lady.

"Of course, I'll pay you for your trouble—even though we didn't really need you." Wincealot's gaze kept straying to the bird. In spite of everything, he felt ashamed, somehow, to see a dragon reduced to this. "I suppose you and my high commissioner have agreed on a fee."

Arnold opened his mouth but made no sound.

The king's voice sounded like the rustle of lizard feet over dry leaves. "You . . . didn't . . . agree . . . on . . . a . . . fee."

"I'll think of something." Brushing past the ruler, the enchanter and the lady strode toward the palace.

The king stepped closer to his brother-in-law, but didn't dare raise his voice. *"You!"*

"It was your idea to send for a sorcerer in the first place."

"But you sent for *this* one."

"Maybe we could have him change the dragon back."

"And double his fee? Besides, you idiot, what would we do with a furious dragon in the palace?"

"It seems to me that after all my work and worry, I've earned more than criticism." Insulted as he was, Arnold, like the king, whispered, for the sorcerer's chimera still stood in the courtyard.

"You have earned . . . you have earned . . ."
Wincealot struggled to keep his voice low. "You
have earned a vacation. A long vacation. Go,
while you still can."

Arnold was outraged. "I'll do that. I'll do just
that."

The king stalked back to the palace, thinking
he would make it a crime for anyone in Minervia
even to speak of sorcerers. First, though, he'd
give this one a generous payment and get rid of
him.

Wincealot found the wizard in the throne
room. From the throne, the thaumaturge regarded the king with glittering eyes. "Nice little
kingdom you have here."

Arnold packed hastily, composing a farewell
note to Dorma in his mind. He wasn't terribly
fond of her, but she was the only blood relative
he had in Minervia, and he felt that someone of
his importance should leave a note for somebody.

He rang for a scribe, but no one came. So.
Cutting off my privileges already, he thought.
Stung, he sat down with a sheaf of rice paper.

Since he'd always used scribes, he'd never
had to learn about spelling and punctuation.
After filling a sheet, he'd written nothing he was
able to read.

He decided to send Dorma a note from
someplace interesting that had scribes.

He rang for a page, but no one came.

Finally, fuming, he carried his own baggage out a back door, just in case the sorcerer's chimera should still be in the courtyard.

At the stables, he rapped sharply on the nearest stall. "What's going on here? Where are the grooms?"

The chimera's lion head rose and swayed toward him.

"Oh. Sorry." Hastily, he retreated to the courtyard, where the stable grooms huddled against the wall, trembling. To his surprise, a white horse stood at the very portals of the palace, shaking its head.

"You." Arnold beckoned the nearest groom. "Get this tired brute out of the courtyard, and then fetch me a decent horse."

"Oh, sir. Please, sir," begged the groom, "don't send me near that thing in the stables."

Arnold was about to reprimand the boy, but he decided not to make a fuss that might disturb the chimera. "All right. Then find a saddle somewhere and put it on this nag."

The horse stood quite still while it was saddled. It seemed dazed, or at least seriously muddled. Arnold would have demanded another steed, but there was not only the chimera to consider. There was Wincealot, who had gone after the sorcerer. Since the king was nowhere in sight, Arnold assumed he was still conferring with Volotor. There no reason to expect that Wincealot would emerge from that meeting in any better humor than he had entered it. Therefore, the most sensible course was to be gone when the king emerged.

Clambering into the saddle, the high commissioner urged the white horse toward the moat.

eight

HE horse was impossible, stopping every few paces to stare back at its rider with a look at once injured, astonished, and dire.

The high commissioner made little progress.

On the third day, the beast turned ugly, rearing and snapping at Arnold.

"It's back to the palace for you, flea bag." The high commissioner hauled on the reins. "It's one thing to be sent on an unexpected vacation, but another to risk my life for it. I'll trade you for a decent steed and be on my way again."

The return journey was a harrowing ordeal, but Arnold maintained a perilous control over the animal.

As they approached the castle, Arnold took some comfort in the expectation that the king, having tried to run Minervia for almost a week, would have had time to regret his waspishness. It wouldn't do to patch things up too quickly—let Wincealot apologize properly before even discussing whether or not the vacation was over.

The drawbridge was already rebuilt and the moat half filled. Work was under way on the ramparts and parapets—it looked as if they were being made even thicker than before.

Arnold stopped at the edge of the moat. Normally, a guard would shout down, " 'oo's there? Wot yer want?" although the high commissioner had almost always been recognized and let in.

Now, however, there was no challenge, no greeting, no sign of life on the battlements. The bridge was lowered by someone unseen, and Arnold's horse clattered across, past the empty sentry boxes outside the castle wall.

The gates opened as they approached. The steed trotted through the gates and across the empty courtyard, stood quietly while Arnold dismounted, and then bit him.

It was hardly fitting for the man who ran Minervia to engage in an altercation with a horse. Since there was nobody in the courtyard to notice them, the high commissioner simply abandoned the beast and hurried into the palace.

"Well, he's done it again." Without so much as a "Welcome back, sir," without a simple "How was your vacation, dear boy?," without even a "You have no idea how desperately you've been missed, H.C.," a noble brushed past Arnold, silver spurs ringing on the marble floor.

"Well, he's done it again." What did the man mean? What kind of greeting was this for the returning high commissioner of Minervia?

Arnold glared after the noble. Could the man be so thick as to have forgotten his own high commissioner in a matter of days? Then a dreadful thought struck Arnold. What if the noble hadn't forgotten him? What if the spur-bearing snob hadn't even noticed his absence? What if nobody had noticed? What if Minervia had been running itself as if the absence of its high commissioner made no difference?

A page hurried by Arnold with barely a glance, muttering distractedly, "Well, he's done it again."

The high commissioner didn't wonder for a moment who had done it. Since Arnold was the only person, aside from Wincealot, who ever did anything worth mentioning, and since Arnold had been on vacation, the king himself must have done whatever it was that had been done.

Dorma came slowly down the great curved staircase, followed by a gaggle of wan, twitterless handmaidens.

"Done what?" he greeted her.

"Uncle Arnold!" Running down the last steps, she threw her arms around him. "I've been so worried! I was afraid something dreadful had happened to you."

He felt her tears soaking his collar. "Done what?" He stepped back, embarrassed by her excessive display of emotion.

She sniffled. "Who?"

"The king, of course. What has he done?"

Her eyes filled with tears again. "Oh, Uncle Arnold, he's done it again."

"DONE WHAT?"

"Didn't you know?" As his face grew red as the trees in her tapestry, she went on hastily, "He's had another noble thrown into the dungeon. That makes six today."

"Good heavens!" Though Arnold was appalled, he couldn't help reflecting that the moment his back was turned, things went to pieces. "Just let some upstarts with their fancy spurs try handling things and the kingdom is overrun with problems, eh?"

"If we're overrun by anything, it's by *him*." Dorma glanced toward the throne room.

Her uncle was shocked. It was one thing to picket the palace, even to get caught in a rock slide with a monster, but she had never spoken disrespectfully of her parents before! "Nobles in the dungeon? For what?"

"For nothing."

"But why?"

"I don't know." Wearily, she leaned against the wall. "Underneath all his evil, I think he's desperately insecure. You know, he invaded Doum this morning, sending those of our knights he hasn't imprisoned."

"Oh, my dear!" Arnold was too stunned by the news to protest the way she vilified her father. "But this means war!"

"Indeed. If anybody notices."

"He was always headstrong and impulsive, but this is too much!"

A shadow fell across them and a chill seemed to snake across the hall. Arnold looked up into glittering green eyes.

The sorcerer's voice was deep and icy as a flooded dungeon. "Didn't I warn you about standing around in drafty halls, princess?"

"Yes."

"Yes, what?"

"Yes, your majesty."

The sorcerer turned his attention to Arnold. "You. Come into the throne room."

There had been changes made in the throne room. On a tall, wide dais stood a massive black iron throne, its arms and legs wrought like twined serpents. Around the walls, green flames hissed in tall black urns.

Seating himself, Volotor looked down at Arnold. "So. What brought you back?"

"A horse."

"You were a high commissioner or something equally useless."

"High commissioner and chief advisor to his majesty, King Wincealot of Minervia. Every proper kingdom has a chief advisor."

"Then you may serve as ours."

Summoning all his courage, Arnold replied, "I serve King Wincealot. Where is he?"

"I've been asking myself the same question. At any rate, he's gone, leaving me king of Minervia."

Overcome with indignation, the high commissioner cried, "Imposter! I demand—demand, I say—to see my king!"

If Wincealot was impulsive, this so-called king was impossible. He pulled on a green scaly cord beside the throne and two guards entered. These were not the simple, sturdy lads who wore those remarkable costumes designed by Dorma's mother. These creatures were dressed in green armor and, so far as Arnold could discern, they were themselves green—hands and faces a pale zucchini, eyes as hard and glittering as emeralds, lips a moldered blackish-green over long jade teeth.

The fleshless fingers that gripped Arnold's arms were so cold they seemed to burn through his sleeves.

"Imposter!" he cried again, though his voice squeaked. "How dare you order the high commissioner of Minervia seized . . .

". . . and *chained* . . .

". . . and thrown into the *dungeon*?"

*   *   *

Clutching the bars of his cell, Arnold whispered, "How dared he?"

"Oh, he dares," hissed the new dungeon keeper, turning the key. "Within hours you will be whimpering, sobbing, begging to apologize to the sorcerer."

"Never!"

He heard the keeper glide away as that "Never!" echoed forlornly through the darkness.

I suppose that last "Imposter!" did it, Arnold thought, sitting on the damp stone floor and wondering how long it would take him to begin whimpering. He heard something move, right there in the cell with him. Sucking in his breath, he huddled against the wall, but the thing came closer.

"Why are you here?" Its voice was low, but human.

"I seem to have offended the sorcerer."

"Sorcerer?"

"He was hired to get rid of our dragon." Arnold felt the cold stone wall against his back.

"He got out, then?"

"Out? He's up there in the throne room."

"The dragon is in the throne room?" Arnold's unseen companion asked.

"No. The sorcerer is in the throne room."

"But what about the dragon? I left it sealed in its cave."

"*You—*"

"Shh. Something's creeping toward our cell!"

"Uncle Arnold?" whispered a soft voice.

"Dorma!" Leaping to his feet, Arnold seized the bars. "Get me out . . ."

"Who's Dorma?" asked his cellmate.

"Who's that?" murmured the princess.

"Miles Bowman. I'm a stranger here."

"Miles! What are you doing in there with my uncle?"

"Your uncle?" The traveler recognized her voice then.

"The high commissioner."

"*You!*" Lithe and fierce despite his imprisonment, the traveler seized the high commissioner.

"What's going *on* in there?" demanded the princess. "What's that scuffling?"

"Help!" Arnold's voice was strained, but sincere.

"Miles! Whatever you're doing, stop! If the sorcerer's guards come and find me here . . ."

As Miles' grip eased, Arnold staggered to his feet and clutched the bars desperately. "My dear," he gasped, *"get me out of here!"*

"I'm afraid it's much easier to get in there, Uncle. When I heard you shouting at Volotor, I guessed where I'd find you next."

"Volotor!" Miles exclaimed.

"You know him?" Dorma asked in amazement.

"Oh, yes." The traveler's voice was bleak now. "He was my friend. His father ruled a kingdom beyond the desert, west of Minervia. My father was Volotor's tutor. When I was ten and

Volotor fifteen, I followed him everywhere. He taught me to swim and ride and fight—even at fifteen, no man could match him. I don't know when, or how, he began to study sorcery. When he was eighteen, his father died, and Volotor's uncle seized the throne. Volotor was silent, but in a few days his uncle simply disappeared and every one of his uncle's supporters fell ill. Volotor proclaimed himself king, but something had happened to him. He'd become as suspicious and secretive as his uncle. He exiled my father, there was a rebellion, and I was arrested. Perhaps because I'd been his friend, Volotor took only my reason, and had me driven from his kingdom. I wandered for years, years I can barely remember."

"So he's done it again." Dorma's voice was low.

"Done what?" Arnold asked, though he felt he should know better.

"My father, too, has disappeared. He hasn't been seen since the night Hugh left."

"Hugh *left*?" Miles interrupted.

"He made a treaty with the dragon," Dorma explained. "He brought the treaty here, but it was rejected, and he was banished."

"*Banished?*" Seizing Arnold by the shoulder, Miles swung him around.

"By the king! It was all the king's doing!" Arnold sputtered, his back against the bars.

"Let him go, Miles!" Dorma commanded.

The traveler's grip eased. "What was the king

thinking of, rejecting treaties, banishing Hugh, inviting a sorcerer into the throne room. Couldn't anyone bring Wincealot to his senses?"

"Miles, no one can *find* him." Dorma's voice was tight. "A few hours after Hugh left, I came downstairs with a plan for delivering the treaty. I found my father gone and the castle overrun with Volotor's creatures. They imprisoned all our knights and disarmed our nobles, and the sorcerer proclaimed himself king of Minervia."

"No one protested?" the high commissioner asked.

"Oh, I did. Volotor had me imprisoned in my chambers. When his guards caught me climbing down the palace wall, he threatened to change me into a newt if I caused any more trouble. He lets me go free within the palace now, so long as I don't catch a chill, but I can find out nothing about my father."

"Volotor knows you're down here?" Arnold asked his niece.

"No, no. This palace, like every proper palace, is honeycombed with secret passages. I spent half my childhood discovering them. Of course, some had been sealed up over the centuries, but you'd be surprised how many that last dragon raid opened. I found one leading from my old nursery to the pantries, another from an abandoned storeroom to this dungeon."

"If the sorcerer worries about your catching a chill," Arnold mused darkly, "it seems likely he intends to force you to marry him."

"I'm terribly afraid he's developed a grudging fondness for me," she admitted. "But fortunately, like everybody else, he tends to disapprove of me. Besides, I don't have a relative free to give me away at any wedding."

"Nor even a mother to counsel you now," Arnold sighed.

"Uncle, you know my father made it treason to mention her."

"But your father is gone," he said.

Dorma began to weep quietly.

The high commissioner reached between the bars to pat her shoulder. "There, there. You mustn't dwell on such sad memories. Let's talk about happier things."

"Hap . . . pap . . . papier things," she sniffled.

They were silent.

Finally, he asked, "How many hours have I been locked up?"

"One, when I came down."

"And all because of that stupid bird."

"Bird?" she asked.

"The dragon."

"Dragon?" She still sounded bewildered.

The knights and nobles in other cells, who'd been listening to the conversation with varying degrees of interest, clustered near their bars now, as confused as the princess.

"The sorcerer changed the dragon to a parrot," Arnold explained, "and for his fee, obviously, he took Minervia."

"Not *Filene's* parrot?" Dorma gasped.

"Filene?" Miles rasped. "The sorcerer's sister, Filene, is here?"

"Well, I certainly didn't want the wretched fowl," Arnold huffed.

Wot they sayin'? asked a knight.

Says the dragon is a parrot.

Tsk. In the gloom, a third knight shook his head, thinking the entire royal family was a bit unsteady.

"Uncle!" Dorma breathed. "If there is any dragon left in that parrot, there's hope. Volotor keeps all the castle master keys constantly with him, but Blys could fly in Volotor's window while he sleeps and bring me the key to unlock the cells and free everyone down here!"

Then wot? came a knight's voice from a dusky cell.

"Then we'll take Volotor by surprise and recapture the palace!" Dorma said.

Wif a set o' keys? came another knight's voice.

And another: *Wot she say now?*

Says we'll take somebody by 'er eyes and rewrap blurry Alice.

Now all the knights and nobles joined in a muted consternation:

Not another charade!

Wot parade?

Did she say the dragon's goin' to bring the keys to let us out?

Bit tight for 'im, these low corridors.

"It's our only chance," the princess assured them.

For wot?

"Freedom! Or would you rather languish in a cell?"

Well . . . wot d'ye think, Gwillam? Languish, or fight them green things and them wavy gray misty types 'o the sorcerer's?

Rile a sorcerer an 'e'll change you into one o' them on the spot, I'll wager.

"The keeper will be coming soon from feeding the crocodiles. I'll be back." Dorma felt she should leave on an inspiring note. "Uh . . . don't lose courage."

nine

ILENE and the hand-maidens, whom she had appropriated from Dorma, were astonished to hear a knock on her door. Nobody came willingly to visit a sorcerer's sister.

One of the hand-maidens opened the door, and Dorma entered.

"What do you want?" Filene hid her surprise.

"I just thought I'd drop by and see if you're comfortable. You'll be much cozier as soon as all the dragon damage is patched up." The princess chatted on as if undisturbed by the lack of response. "Unusual parrot." She peered into the cage. "Does it talk?"

"Leave it alone," Filene snapped.

"It seems depressed."

"Only sulking."

"I think it's sick. I'm awfully good with birds. Let me see what I can do . . ."

"Stay away from it or I'll have you changed to an earwig."

As Filene tossed a cloth over the cage, the princess caught the sleeve of the sorceress's hooded gown.

"Oops. Sorry—I thought you had a thread hanging."

"Idiot! You've ripped my sleeve."

"I'll have it mended. I'll even have pearls embroidered over the tear."

"You will not have it mended." Filene beckoned for handmaidens to help her out of the gown. Then she threw it to Dorma. "You'll mend it yourself, by morning. Is that clear?"

Dorma nodded. Clasping the gown, she hurried from Filene's chamber, shutting the door firmly behind her.

On her way to her own chambers, she dropped into her former handmaidens' rooms and borrowed a few more things.

Though he'd gone from four-ton reptile to a mere parrot, from shock to terror to despair, Blys was still a dragon inside. Humans had made him nervous when he was seventy times their size; now he found them even more unsettling—and he was in no position to act upon his prejudices.

Though he had ruffled his feathers when

Dorma stood before his cage, he hadn't missed how quickly she'd unfastened the latch on the cage door.

After the princess had left, Filene went into an inner chamber to practice unspeakable spells, and the handmaidens went to their rooms.

Blys nudged the cage door.

Dragon wings were not intended for flying, but for balance and intimidation. As he stepped out of the cage, he fluttered the strange new feathered wings only out of nerves.

Before he realized what had happened, he had flown off the table.

Once he got over the shock of realizing he could fly, his first thoughts, naturally, were of wrecking the palace and terrorizing anyone handy. He realized, however, that he was still a parrot, not even large enough to terrorize a hare. Even if he could fly to his lair, he'd hardly be a match for archers, knights, or, heaven forfend, sacrifices!

The only hope was that Dorma had some good reason for releasing him. He jittered around the room a bit, then flew out. He wobbled, he tumbled, he yawed, but he managed to circle the palace walls before he clutched a vine near an open window and clung, gathering his composure. He could see into a large chamber. On a bed, eyes closed, lay a tall, pale man.

Barely suppressing a yawp of terror, the bird fluttered away.

Then he saw, below and to his left, a hand waving from an open casement.

"Thank heaven!" Dorma greeted him as he flew into her room. "Blys, I've got a plan. You won't like the part about freeing the knights. . . . Wait! Wait! Isn't it better than being a parrot the rest of your life? Volotor, the sorcerer who transformed you . . . *Will* you settle down and listen? Volotor keeps all the castle's master keys with him. Candles burn in his window all night, and shadows move, so he must sleep in the daytime. Surely sorcerers sleep. He spends the hours just before supper in his chambers, with no one in the palace allowed to make a sound, so it must be then. And then is now."

Blys was edgy, and he'd eaten nothing but seeds for days, but he was eager to do whatever had to be done.

"You must fly in his window and get those keys for me. Of course it's . . ."

He darted from her room before he could lose his nerve . . . or the sorcerer awaken.

". . . a dreadful risk . . ." she finished lamely.

Blys flew to the wizard's window.

Inside, the man still slept. On a chair beside him were glossy green robes, shoes, and three keys on a ring.

His heart fluttering against the cage of his ribs, Blys flew into the chamber and seized the keys.

They were heavier than he expected. Struggling to keep aloft, he flew back to Dorma's chamber and dropped them.

Half an hour later, the princess appeared at the dungeon door, her face hidden by the hood of Filene's gown, the parrot on her shoulder. "Guards, my brother wants you at once, out on the tournament field. I will look after the prisoners."

Nobody lagged when the sorceress commanded.

With the keepers gone, Dorma hurried to Arnold's cell. "Uncle? Take heart." She fumbled with the keys.

At last, the door opened, groaning.

The princess hurried to the next cell.

'ere! Wot yer doin'? demanded a knight's voice as she began to unlock the door.

"Freeing you to overthrow the sorcerer," she told him.

There was a rustling throughout the dungeon as prisoners withdrew to the rear of their cells.

"Knights and nobles of Minervia!" she addressed them in clear, ringing tones. "Who will join me in reclaiming our beloved kingdom?"

When the silence became embarrassing, she said, "All right. We'll escape now and rally later. As soon as we're out of the palace, some of you will slip into the stables . . ."

Escape a dungeon jus' ter move into a stable?

"No, no. To get horses," she explained.

Eeyew! You seen wot's in the stables? That gordon!

"You mean gorgon," said Miles, beside the princess. "Gordon is a man's name."

"I think he means gargoyle," Arnold suggested. "A gorgon is a snake-haired hag."

"A gargoyle is a carved monster. He must mean gryphon," Dorma said.

'e means that thing the sorcerer rides. Catch me near that!

Dorma sighed. "You mean the chimera. All right. We'll escape now and then get horses from the village. I'll go first."

'ow come royalty always gets to go first?

With an effort, she kept her temper. "Because, wearing Filene's gown, with Filene's parrot, when I reach the castle wall and the parrot flies over it, I'll shout, 'Lower the drawbridge! My dragon's escaping!' The guards, thinking I'm the sorceress, will obey, and we'll all rush . . ."

Wot parrot?

The one on 'er shoulder. You can jus' make it out.

The parrot that's a dragon?

SHE'S GONE AND BROUGHT A DRAGON DOWN 'ERE!

Unable to still the pandemonium, the princess threw the keys into the next cell, shouted instructions, and ran, Miles and Arnold with her, to the secret passage she'd used the last time.

They crawled through burrows and tunnels, channels and conduits, until they emerged at last in her old nursery. Shoving aside a picnic hamper she'd packed, she began pulling clothes out of a chest. "Put these on."

"Are those ladies' garments?" Arnold asked uneasily.

"A few things I borrowed," Dorma said.

"I would rather die than wear ladies' garments!" her uncle declared hotly.

"I would rather wear them than die," Miles said. "And we'd better be far from here before Volotor discovers what Dorma's done."

Filene's hood close around her face, Blys on her shoulder, the princess led Arnold and Miles, dressed in handmaidens' gowns, down back stairways to the ground level of the palace. "Volotor keeps all but the front portals locked," she told them, "so we have to cross the great hall. But the court is at supper now."

They were nearly across the hall when they heard, above them, a scream like an enraged eagle's. "My gown! Dorma, you cat!" As Filene scrambled down the staircase, the handmaidens close behind her recognized their belongings and erupted in a chorus of outrage.

"My veil!"

"My wimple!"

"*My word!*" The high commissioner bolted for the portals, Miles and Dorma close behind.

As they burst into the courtyard, a white horse reared, snorting. Then, recognizing Arnold, it charged.

"Beast! Brute! Anarchist!" Shouting abuse at the horse, Arnold sprinted for the castle wall.

"Blys, fly!" the princess panted as they neared the sentry boxes.

With the bird winging toward Volotor's guards, she shouted, "Open the gates! Lower the drawbridge! My dragon's escaping!"

They obeyed. Not even Volotor's creatures would dare upset his sister. And not even green guards would willingly interfere with a departing dragon.

The horse gnashing at Arnold's heels, the fugitives dashed through the gates and across the drawbridge.

In the courtyard, Filene stopped, handmaidens piling up behind her. "It's no use. They're too far ahead."

From behind her came a voice so deep, so cold, that the handmaidens quailed. "I assume there is a reason for this tumult, Filene?"

Volotor had slept his usual few hours, then risen to dress for dinner, only to find the castle's master keys missing. He ordered dinner held, but he was, for the first time in his life, confounded. A sorcerer, proud and fierce, utterly controlled, accustomed to holding kingdoms in a grip of terror, he could hardly admit to misplacing a whole set of keys, so there was no way he could have the palace searched for them.

Descending the stairs in a grim humor, he was assailed by the clamor of the pursuit. "I assume there is a reason," he repeated.

"The princess Dorma," Filene told him, "has left us, with two persons who are dressed as handmaidens, and who run like no handmaidens I've ever seen."

"Guards!" Her brother's fury was so terrible the handmaidens drew closer together and even the green guards, who came running, cringed.

Volotor ordered all the castle searched.

The guards who went through the dungeons discovered the door of Miles and Arnold's cell open. Other guards found the dungeon keepers stolidly waiting at the tournament field where Dorma had sent them.

The knights and nobles in the other cells stood quietly, admiring themselves for having had the good sense not to escape.

When the guards reported to Volotor, he commanded in a voice like black frost, "Bring the hunting jackals."

They were brought, great gaunt grinning beasts with spotted tawny hides. With them came Volotor's trackers, before whom even the green guards lowered their eyes. They resembled men, these trackers, but they resembled, more, gray wraiths, frost smoke. Sometimes, when a shaft of light struck one, it seemed to pass right through him.

"And the hunting hawks."

Those bloody birds, birds so dreadful only the sorcerer dared release them, were brought in iron cages mounted on war platforms.

Volotor did not hurry. His jackals, like the trackers, would lope for days following the trail, while above them the hawks would soar, golden eyes missing nothing below. The prey would have to eat, and drink, and rest.

Volotor knew how such hunts ended.

This was not his first.

ten

NJOYING Arnold's rout far too much to end it quickly, the white horse pursued him, snorting.

Finally, though, the high commissioner tripped on the hem of the gown he was wearing, and the horse reared above him, snorting.

"That's enough of *that*!" Dorma smacked it sharply on the flank.

With a *fwoomph* of astonishment, it came down on all four hooves, baring its teeth at her.

"You either behave yourself or we turn you back for the sorcerer to find," she warned.

The effect on the beast was dramatic. It pawed the earth, rolling its eyes, but they both understood that it would give no more trouble— at least while she was watching.

"What do you call this noble steed?" she

asked her uncle to soothe the animal's feelings a bit.

Arnold sat up. "It's just a horse."

"Very well. Horse, we're depending on you. If we all come through this, I will have a statue of you erected in the castle courtyard."

She had gauged the beast's vanity acutely. Shaking its mane, it struck a resolute pose.

"I suppose we should travel at night and hide during the day." Arnold stood, keeping a wary eye on Horse.

"It makes no difference," Miles said. "Volotor's creatures see in dark as well as light. We'd better keep going as long as we can."

"Where?" Slipping out of the handmaiden's gown, Arnold brushed off his velvet knee britches and straightened the cuffs of his shirt.

"I brought a map." Leading them into the shelter of an olive grove, Dorma set down the hamper of provisions purloined from the palace pantries and unrolled the map on the ground. "Minervia, as you see, is shaped like—"

"A blob," Miles said.

"Yes, rather. And we're about—"

"Here." Miles put his finger on the map. "Precisely on the purple patch."

She glanced at him. "Yes. Now, west of Minervia is—"

"Desert," the traveler said, "empty of life, scourged by ceaseless sandstorms. And beyond that, the land which Volotor rules."

Dorma nodded a trifle brusquely. "Then, to the south of Minervia is—"

"Swamp," he said, "sinister, sulphurous, quivering with quagmires and quicksand."

"To the north—" she went on, an edge to her voice.

"Is a vast wasteland, and beyond it a country swept by perpetual tempests, so wild it's never been mapped."

"*Finally*, to the east—"

"Are mountains. With three good horses, we might cross them in a matter of days. And beyond the mountains, Doum."

"Our only chance," Arnold said. "Visitors to or from Minervia always travel by way of Doum."

"Uncle," Dorma reminded him, "Volotor has invaded Doum. It may be part of Minervia by now."

In the seeping twilight, Arnold peered at the map. "Desert, swamp or wasteland—"

"Are impossible," Miles told him. "Impassable."

"You're sure?" Arnold persisted.

"Absolutely. I crossed them."

"How?" Arnold asked.

"Burning with fever, trembling with chills, starving, raving from thirst."

"The mountains, then." Arnold strove to keep his voice steady. "All we have to do is keep ahead of Volotor's pursuit, elude his armies, and convince the Prince of Doum that we're fugitives, not spies."

They traveled east, keeping to the shelter of orchards and vineyards where they could, until the twilight was swallowed by night.

"We must seek out some hermit's humble hut and beg shelter for a few hours," Arnold said.

"Uncle," Dorma muttered, "would you put any Minervian in the position of aiding enemies of Volotor?"

"Or of refusing to tell the sorcerer where we'd gone?" Miles added.

They blundered through the dark until they saw ahead a deeper, looming blackness.

"Forest," Dorma said. "We can rest there until first light."

Entering the night forest was like being engulfed in a dream. All around them were the muted converse and swift secret movements of unseen creatures. Then they heard, almost at their feet, the cheerful, mindless plashing of a stream. They stopped to drink, and to rest.

The first questioning bird calls woke them. It was that soft hour before dawn when every sound seems to come from some far place, every movement seems slowed, and a kind of mist seems to render every object insubstantial.

As they made their way between the trees, dew-damped leaves strayed over their faces, branchlets plucked at them, even roots seemed to clutch at their feet, as if imploring them to stay in the cool green shelter of the woods.

They emerged from the forest's eastern fringe onto an eerie, desolate plain of black, almost glassy rock, dotted with the twisted skeletons of trees. As they hurried toward the eastern mountains, the sound of their passage seemed magnified, while all around them was a waiting silence, as if, just out of sight, some great beast crouched with massive paw uplifted. In the flat, pale sky a cold white disc of sun swam.

Something passed in a rush, just overhead.

Miles looked up. "Hawk," he said, gently loosening the parrot's talons, which had tightened convulsively on his shoulder.

Dorma glanced back toward the forest.

The western sky was filled with dark wings, making a sort of moving canopy for the sorcerer, who rode forward surrounded by his hunters.

The fugitives stumbled toward the eastern range. Its cliffs were shrouded in a dark mist. An icy wind screamed down through a pass to claw across the plain.

Volotor and his hunting party were rapidly closing the distance between them and their quarry, the trackers moving as silently, as effortlessly, as the loping jackals.

Dorma and her companions hurried toward the pass.

There emerged from the mist, blocking their way, a towering figure in black armor seated on a black stallion. It was an image from epics, from ballads, from nightmares—the dread Black Knight of Doum.

110

The dragon huddled, trembling, in Miles' arms.

It was Arnold who recovered first. "Although we've never met, noble sir, I know you by reputation."

"Glorious reputation," Dorma added hastily.

"I wonder if you'd mind terribly permitting us to pass to the pass, Your Worthiness," Arnold asked.

The knight, who was followed by a minstrel dressed in gold and scarlet, looked down at Arnold and Dorma, then past them toward Volotor and his hunting party.

Guiding his stallion around the fugitives, the man in black rode toward Volotor. "You are the leader of this group?"

The sorcerer rode forward alone, reining his chimera a few feet from the knight. "I am Volotor, Emperor of Minervia."

"Yesterday he was merely king," Dorma observed. "See how he's always promoting himself?"

"I bring a message to Minervia from the Prince of Doum." Even muffled by his visor, the knight's voice carried like the low rumble of approaching thunder.

"Deliver it, then," the sorcerer said.

"It is for the rightful ruler of Minervia."

The sorcerer was calm. "I am presently the only ruler."

The knight gazed at him, then at his forces. "So it would seem. The prince condemns your unprovoked invasion of Doum, but he would spare both countries the tragedy of a prolonged war. He challenges you to name a champion, one man to meet the champion he names to fight for Doum. The outcome of that battle will determine—"

"I will consider the challenge after I attend to the matter at hand." The sorcerer attempted to ride forward, but the knight blocked his way. "This lady and her companions are . . . were . . . my guests," Volotor said. "I intend to escort them back to my palace."

"That is for them to decide," the knight said. "They are under my protection now."

The sorcerer surveyed his waiting forces and the hawks circling overhead. He smiled.

"You and I can settle our disagreement now," the knight said. "I offer you the same challenge the Prince of Doum offers. Name a champion from among your . . . legions. When I defeat him, you and your followers may retreat unharmed, leaving this lady and her companions to go where they will."

The wizard's smile was as cold as a serpent's heart. "And if you lose?"

"I never lose."

"Knight, you stand in great need of humbling."

"Name your champion."

The sorcerer pointed at Arnold. "That."

"Don't mock me, Volotor." The knight's voice was low and terrible.

A pale light flickered in the sorcerer's eyes. "Your arrogance invites mockery, knight. You have interfered with me, challenged me, and very nearly annoyed me. I can think of nothing that will cause you deeper, longer suffering than a wound to your outrageous pride. It will amuse me to see you atone in this way for your impertinence. Of course, if you refuse to fight my chosen champion, you stand forfeit, dishonored, and I am free to claim my . . . guests."

"Suppose I end all this quibbling by passing up the honor," Arnold suggested.

"Then you will be turned into a toadstool," the sorcerer replied crisply.

"Volotor . . ." The knight's voice was vibrant with rage.

"Wait!" Dorma called. "Knight, we must speak with you."

The knight hesitated, then guided his charger back to where she stood.

"You must see you're dealing with a sorcerer," she told him. "You've stung Volotor into trying to humiliate you, fortunately. You can defeat my uncle here without damaging him, and save us all. Or you can goad the sorcerer into real anger, and not even you will escape."

"She's right," Miles said.

"Excellent analysis," the high commissioner agreed. "Pity I have no sword."

The knight passed his sheathed sword to the high commissioner.

"It's rather heavy for me," Arnold protested. "And, of course, I'm still lacking a lance."

The man in black handed down his lance. "Where's your armor?"

"I rented it out some time ago." The high commissioner glowered at Miles.

"No armor?" The knight hesitated briefly, then dismounted. "What do you need?"

"A shield would be useful," Miles said quickly, "and your mail, the chest and back plates, arm and leg guards . . ."

The knight took off all the items Miles mentioned and gave them to Arnold, who glanced at the watching wizard and then accepted them.

Touching a lute, the knight's minstrel sang in a clear, high voice:

Compelled by courtly chivalry,
The knight gave up both sword and lance,
And stood unarmored, shivery
In helmet, shirt and flimsy . . .

"Please!" Arnold sniffed, and the minstrel was silent.

As Miles buckled him into the armor, the high commissioner said, "He's showing his scorn, giving me all this. It's his way of demonstrating that he can defeat me bare-handed."

"No," Dorma murmured. "He's furious that Volotor is mocking him. It's his way of showing contempt for the sorcerer."

114

"Don't you want the helmet, too?" Miles asked.

"I can barely stand inside all this iron as it is. If he so much as sneezes, I'll collapse like a pile of pots. Besides, I don't *want* to see his face."

"Just remember, Uncle, that his vanquishing you is our only hope," Dorma said.

"Ready?" the knight asked as the wind from the mountains cut through his black muslin shirt.

Arnold staggered, clanking, toward Horse. As the beast skittered backward, Miles caught the reins. "Try to escape, nag," he growled, "and Volotor's jackals will bring you down in a second."

Horse rolled his eyes wildly, but stood while Miles and Dorma boosted Arnold into the saddle.

The man in black blew on numb fingers.

"Look at him, cool as a crocodile. He knows I'm no match for him, even now." The high commissioner watched the knight vault easily into the saddle.

"When I lift my hand," Volotor announced, "begin. If either of you is unhorsed, you will fight on foot, to the death."

"The *death*?" The princess went pale.

"Oh, come now!" Arnold protested. "Couldn't we make it to something less—"

"*To the death!*" The sorcerer lifted his hand.

As the knight's black charger thundered toward Horse, Dorma cried, "Volotor!" but there was no halting the contest now.

Arnold jabbed at the knight with the lance,

but the man in black ducked under the thrust and with his bare fist struck Arnold's shield such a blow that the high commissioner was thrown from the saddle. Horse, glancing at the black stallion, then at the chimera, stopped and stood perfectly still.

Arnold landed on his back with a crashing like all the cymbals in the royal orchestra being thrown down a staircase. As he lay trapped in the oversize armor, the knight leaped from his charger and strode to him. Though Arnold was half stunned, the phrase "To the death!" rang in his mind. Snaking out a mailed hand, he seized his opponent's ankle and yanked hard.

Outraged by this breach of chivalry, the knight twisted as he fell, landing like an angry lion on the high commissioner.

Horse averted his gaze, like one who is determined to ignore an ugly scene.

Arnold kicked, clawed, even bit, but the other gripped him by the throat and rasped, "Yield!"

"He yields!" Dorma cried. "He does! I saw him!"

"He's turning blue!" Miles warned.

Releasing Arnold, the knight stood and turned to Volotor. "Now, sorcerer . . ."

"I said to the death."

The knight stepped toward him with the grace of a stalking panther. "So you said, haruspex, but that was not part of *my* agreement. There is nothing in the rules of combat that requires a knight to accept a foe who trips him, bites and kicks. Am I to tell the Prince of Doum that Minervia is ruled by a shabby wizard who has no conception of honor, whose idea of a champion is a clownish knave who rents out his own armor?"

"The knight has won." Miles' voice was cold and clear. "His conditions stand unless, Volotor, you choose to show yourself as even more contemptible than I know you to be."

For the first time, the sorcerer looked closely at the traveler. "You!" he whispered. "You . . . have changed."

"I survived. And you have been defeated by this champion."

"Defeated?" The pupils of the sorcerer's eyes narrowed and wavered like flames in a wind, and he glanced at the knight. "Suppose we . . . negotiate."

The man in black stepped closer to the chimera. "And what could you and I have to discuss?"

"Why, peace, my boy, peace."

"Peace requires, first, your immediate withdrawal." The knight rested one hand on the chimera's neck.

"Reasonable. Entirely reasonable. I'll send my hunting party away at once, except for a few faithful servants. Then we can talk. We might discuss all the Minervian knights and nobles in our dungeons."

"To say nothing of King Wincealot." Struggling to his knees, Arnold managed to seize Horse's reins and haul himself to a standing position.

Volotor looked closely at Horse then, and the flicker of surprise that passed over his face was erased by a glint of amusement. "To say nothing of Wincealot," he said.

"You swear to harm no one, sorcerer?" the knight demanded.

"To harm no one."

"Send back your forces, then."

When the hunting party had withdrawn, Volotor dismounted. "This looks like a pleasant place to set up a conference tent. To work, few faithful servants."

In minutes, the sorcerer's retainers set up a silk tent, scattered velvet cushions on soft-napped rugs, then padded silently back and forth, brewing tea over copper basins of charcoal and serving it in porcelain cups.

While the knight and Volotor talked in low voices, the minstrel sang:

The Black Knight, all of sable hue,
Feared by all and known by few . . .

"Aha!" Arnold whispered to Miles. "The Black Knight's name is Sable!"

"*Sable?*" Miles looked dubious.

"Aren't you listening to the ballad? *The Black Knight, all of sable hue . . .*"

Miles knew it was ridiculous to argue, but the distraction eased the temptation to attack Volotor in the middle of a peace talk. "Sable is another word for black, just as hue is another

118

word for color. You might as well say his name is hue."

Dorma leaned closer. "Who?"

"No, hue," Miles said.

She half rose from where she sat. *"Hugh?"*

Turning toward her, the knight removed his helmet.

He was even more impressive without it.

His hair was thick and straight, as black as his burnished armor. His eyes were the deep gray of storm clouds, his face stern, proud and somber.

"Hugh!" Miles and Dorma cried at once.

The parrot let out a yawp of astonishment.

"What are you doing here, peasant?" Arnold demanded.

Hugh set the helmet on the rug beside him. "After Wincealot banished me, I made my way to Doum, a few days ahead of Minervia's troops. When I heard of the invasion, I thought Wincealot must have lost his senses. I went to the Prince of Doum, who had no idea I was Minervian, of course, and suggested he challenge Wincealot to name a champion. Having observed Minervian knights in action, I assumed that, whoever Wincealot named, there would be a very brief combat with no real damage."

"You are Minervian?" the sorcerer asked.

Hugh nodded. "As the Black Knight of Doum, carrying the Prince's message," he said to Dorma, "I could return to my own country without being thrown into its dungeons."

119

"But what happened to the real Black Knight of Doum?" Arnold asked.

"I am he."

"Oh, come off it," Arnold scoffed. "You're a farmer's son."

"And sent up to the dragon many years ago," Hugh said. "Even then, I couldn't help noticing that there were no children of knights or nobles among the sacrifices. When the dragon threw me out, I wandered, without money or provisions or friends. Remembering who was sacrificed and who wasn't, I tagged after any knights I came across. I learned, I practiced, and I acquired, along with scars, a certain ferocity and skill. I won a few tournaments, and then the great tournament at Doum, where I was knighted for valor. Finally, I came home to Minervia, hoping I'd been away long enough to be welcome. I left my armor in Doum—you don't come home only to be challenged by every knight who wants to make a name for himself, only to spend your visit trouncing your countrymen."

"The Black Knight of Doum a Minervian," Volotor said softly.

There was a flash, a blinding radiance, and the tent seemed engulfed in light.

Then darkness.

Dorma heard her own voice calling from a great distance. The blackness faded to a cold light, and she saw that she was in a tower room of the

120

palace. The green guard who brought her food and water would answer none of her questions.

On the second day, Filene came to the room. "Are you trying to starve yourself? You haven't eaten a thing."

"What has Volotor done to—"

"If you don't eat, you'll make yourself sick."

"What happened to the others?"

"And if you're sick, you're useless." The sorceress set the bird cage on a table. "Miserable parrot bit me. I've a notion to turn it into—"

"Filene!"

"I don't know whether you or it unlatched the cage door last time, but thanks to that I'm ordered to keep my eye on the beastly fowl constantly. Oh . . . my brother wants you."

Carrying the cage, Filene escorted Dorma down to the throne room, which was filled with haggard nobles, wan ladies, green guards, the sorcerer, and the prisoners.

"You swore, Volotor." Hugh's voice was hard. "You swore to harm no one."

"And who is harmed?" The wizard sat on the black serpent-throne, his eyes reflecting the green flames that illumined the room. "Doum has declared war," he told the court, "and challenges us to name one man to fight for all Minervia." He gazed at Hugh. "Since you seem so fond of this kind of contest, I've chosen you our champion."

"*Yours?*"

"Certainly. You're a Minervian, the most formidable knight of our times, and, as you mentioned earlier, you never lose."

"After you put me through that shameful farce with the high commissioner . . ."

"That was to amuse myself and chasten you a bit, and I knew I'd do as I wished, whatever the outcome. But this is serious."

"You think I would fight for you?"

"For Minervia, then. And to prevent the princess from becoming, say, a cricket." He lifted a hand. "I wouldn't harm her for the world. Only a simple transformation. You may think it over in the dungeon, knight."

After green guards led Hugh away, Volotor turned his attention to the minstrel. "Look at you. You're a disgrace. What's your name?"

"Leila."

Arnold wondered how he could have missed noticing that the slight, exquisite being was, indeed, female.

"What are you doing dressed up like a troubadour and trailing after a knight?" the sorcerer demanded. "What would your parents think?"

"They think I'm a disgrace. But it's not their fault."

"Oh?" he raised an eyebrow.

"I led a sheltered life in a noble household in Doum until one day, as I was playing my lute in the garden, a dread crimea carried me away."

"You mean a chimera," the sorcerer told her.

"I think she means a centaur," Miles ventured. "Centaurs are half man, half horse, and have a reputation for carrying off maidens."

"Or maybe a cyclops," Dorma suggested. "Cyclopes are one-eyed giants with barbarous manners."

"Or a colossus," Arnold said.

"A colossus," Miles told the high commissioner brusquely, "is only an enormous statue."

"I was carried off by a creature much like that thing you ride," Leila told the wizard.

"Oh, one of *those*," Filene said. "Go on."

"As it carried me over the wall, I realized a sheltered life is no protection at all." Leila looked at the sorcerer solemnly. "Nobody came to save me. I was too shocked to eat or drink, so I was shriveling away when the Black Knight rescued me and sent the beast into oblivion."

"Oblivion," Arnold said. "If I remember my geography, that would be somewhere north of—"

"He took me back to my family," Leila went on, "but I escaped and followed him."

"Escaped from your *family*?" Volotor asked sternly.

"Once you've been carried off by a . . . whatever . . . you want to stay around the only person who saved you," she explained.

The sorcerer regarded her inscrutably.

"But he took me back to my family again," she continued, "left his armor with us, and returned to Minervia. You lead a sheltered life, and everybody tells you some day a wonderful man will come along and take you away to live happily ever after, so you do everything you're told, and you're taken away by a monster instead. The wonderful man comes, but he doesn't want you. I was beginning to question a lot of things, when he returned to claim his armor. This time I disguised myself as a minstrel and followed him, through mud and wind and cold and hardship. Miserable life, a knight's is."

The wizard's voice was low. "Foolish maiden. Why didn't you go home?"

"And leave him to face all that alone, after he'd rescued me?" She was silent then, thoughtful and bewildered.

Volotor regarded her for a long time. Finally he said, "Filene, get her cleaned up and dressed decently and fed." He glanced at Dorma. "Both of them. Meanwhile, this high commissioner and I will prepare a reply for Doum."

Filene led Dorma and Leila from the throne room.

Arnold was escorted to the council chamber and seated at a long table with a supply of pens and ink and parchment. Behind him, Volotor paced. "Take this down. 'To the Prince of Doum: We are in receipt of yours of the twelfth . . .' "

As the sorcerer dictated, the high commissioner scribbled frantically. Interrupting the sorcerer or disobeying him, Arnold knew, would hardly be wise. There was no harm in doing a little writing in order to avoid the dungeons.

At last, Volotor stopped pacing. "Read it back to me."

"What?"

"Read back what I said."

So Arnold was returned to the dungeon after all.

Filene took the two women to her own chambers. For a time she stood at her window, staring out. Then she turned. "We can't let him suffer any more. He is too brave, too noble. We must save him."

Astonished as she was, still Dorma thought fast. "If we save anybody, we save everybody. All of them."

Filene pondered for a moment. "I suppose you're right. He's too honorable to let us save him and not the others. While my brother is preparing his reply to Doum, I'll put a sleeping spell on the guards and grooms and the rest of the court. While I let the men out of their cells, you get six horses ready. Has either of you ever saddled a horse?"

"Dozens of times," Leila said. "That's part of following a wandering knight."

"You'll have to work fast. Sleeping spells don't last."

"What about the chimera?" Dorma asked.

"Don't worry. Give me half an hour, then go to the stables."

Neither Leila nor the princess could open the new lock on the door of the parrot cage. Finally, carrying the cage, they hurried out of the palace and to the stables.

As they picked their way around slumbering grooms, Dorma said, "We must find Horse. He's not much use, but I can't bear to leave him. Then we can find Hugh's stallion . . ."

Both animals were in the stables.

"Can you hurry?" Dorma urged, hoisting the fourth saddle for Leila.

"Hurry!" came a whisper from outside.

Dorma led Horse and the black stallion from the stables, Leila following with two chargers.

The sorceress was waiting. "Only four? What have you been doing?"

"I'll get two more, but it's not easy working with a chimera snoring practically beside you," Leila murmured.

"Four mounts will do," Hugh said.

Miles nodded. "Hurry now, Filene. When your brother finds his guards sleeping, he'll know—"

"I've risked myself to save you," the sorceress said furiously. "If you think I'm going to let you not escape—"

"Volotor would only track us all down again," Hugh told her. "With the guards asleep and him unsuspecting, we have a poor chance, but the best we'll ever have."

"Where are the weapons stored?" Miles asked Dorma.

"Idiots!" Filene raged. "I command you to escape!"

Though her voice was not loud, it was fierce enough to rouse the drowsing chimera. From the stables came a hissing, then a roar, then a scream that made even Hugh's stallion rear. With a splintering of wood, the chimera shattered its stall and came hurtling toward the sounds it had heard.

"Down, you brute!" commanded the sorceress.

But, as she had pointed out, sleeping spells don't last. The green guards, already stirring, were roused by the commotion. Within moments they swarmed over beasts and humans, and then the trackers, silent, relentless, engulfed the area.

By the time Volotor arrived, the battle was over.

"I thought you'd never come!" Filene told her brother. "Here I was, all by myself, trying to prevent their escape."

"Bring them to the throne room," the sorcerer told his creatures. "Then wake the court."

eleven

"LEEPING, my master," hissed the green guard. "The grooms, trackers, jackals, palace guards, dungeon guards, all sleeping."

The sorcerer gripped the iron arms of the throne as if he were in pain. *"Filene . . ."*

"It was only a simple spell," Dorma said quickly. "I never dabble in anything dangerous."

Volotor very nearly showed surprise. "You?" He looked at the handmaidens. "Is this true?"

"Well, there are rumors," one whispered, transfixed by that terrible voice and too terrified to lie to the wizard. "She has been known to read privately."

Gazing at Dorma with admiration, Volotor said, "You are . . . fascinating, Princess. But far too troublesome to be left free. By violating my hospitality you have all released me from my pledge to do you no harm."

"Volotor," Miles interrupted, "you are a

bully, a fool, and a second-rate sorcerer. In front of all this court, I challenge you . . ."

". . . to a fair fight on the field of honor." Hugh spoke with difficulty, for the wounds he'd gotten from green guards and trackers had not yet been tended. "And if you refuse, you show yourself before everyone here to be a coward, afraid to face a man with only a man's weapons."

"Don't interrupt!" Dorma whispered, seizing her uncle's arm. "I told you Volotor is insecure. If they can shame him into forgoing sorcery for even a little while, they may have a chance."

"Have you learned nothing from years of madness?" the enchanter asked Miles. "And you, knight, you are gravely wounded."

"Then you may be almost a match for me," Hugh said.

The sorcerer regarded him coldly. "I will begin with you, then. We meet on the tournament field at dawn."

"On foot," Miles said. "No chimera, no Horse."

Volotor nodded. Then he gazed at Leila. "And you may make a ballad of the combat. What do you say to that?"

When she didn't reply, he leaned toward her. "Speak."

"She can't speak," Filene snapped. "She hasn't made a sound since your stupid crimea attacked us."

"You mean my chimera."

"A person might recover from such an encounter once, but twice is unspeakable."

"She can't talk?" the sorcerer asked.

"Not a word," Filene assured him.

"Why didn't she say so? Call in the royal physicians."

"After a fright like she had? Physicians, magicians, warlocks, they're all the same."

"Go mix her a potion," the sorcerer told his sister.

"It could make her sick."

"Then test it on the princess. Go!"

Filene took Dorma's arm.

"And get that bird cage out of the throne room," he added.

The sorceress was silent as she climbed the stairs to her chambers. She kicked open her door and, when she'd shut it behind them, fumed, "I should give up on you all. Challenging Volotor to combat! As if the only art he's mastered is sorcery." Striding across the room, she unlocked an inner door.

Dorma followed her into a small, cold cubicle. The shadows in the corners seemed almost solid, and the things on the shelves that lined the walls made Dorma shiver.

Setting the parrot cage on the floor, Filene rummaged among jars and phials. "Tail of newt . . . mandrake root . . . chimney soot . . . demon's boot . . ."

"Could you put a spell on Volotor?" Dorma asked.

"My own brother?" The sorceress almost dropped a cruet.

"I'm not talking about anything permanent."

"Put that thought right out of your mind. He could slap a counterspell on any enchanter alive." With her sleeve, Filene swept a clear space on a dusty, cluttered table.

"Even if he had no warning? What I'm thinking is that once he starts to wonder how I distributed a sleeping spell when you were supposed to be watching me . . ."

"One more word and I'll change you to a sea slug!"

Muttering to herself, the sorceress pulverized and measured and mixed, and finally poured a hissing, foaming liquid into a golden goblet. "Try it."

"Me?" Dorma drew back.

"Oh, don't be silly. It can't hurt you. It only . . . reverses certain conditions."

"Would it hurt the parrot?"

"No, it would not hurt the parrot," Filene snapped.

"Then try it on him."

The sorceress' glare was so menacing Dorma took the goblet and sipped from it. *"Yick."*

"Good. That's how it's supposed to taste." Taking the goblet in both hands, Filene said, "Bring the bird. Volotor wants none of you left unattended for a moment, now. You lead the way, and if you make me spill a drop of the potion, I'll . . ."

131

Never taking her eyes from the chalice, the enchantress felt her way cautiously out of her chambers and down the stairs after Dorma.

As they approached the tournament field, they heard the ring of metal on metal. Dorma hesitated, and the sorceress nearly walked into her.

"You clod!" Filene cried, never taking her eyes from the goblet. "You almost made it splash!" But her voice trembled.

Silent, frightened ladies and nobles filled the front rows of the stands facing the field, and on the royal platform Leila stood, flanked by green guards.

In the clear morning light, black pennants bearing the green serpent sign of Volotor glistened and moved, though there was no breeze.

On that unkempt field, the contest had already begun.

Though the man in black fought with a courage that brought tears to the eyes of the lords and ladies watching, the sorcerer was as swift and deadly as a serpent's strike.

The black armor was heavy and cumbersome, slowing its wearer, making his footing even more uncertain on the wet and rutted field.

The sorcerer's chain mail was so intricately crafted it moved with his body like a fine silk. His sword was slender, but it found each jointure, each gap in the black armor. While the sorcerer avoided the other man's every thrust, his own blade drew blood again and again.

Driven inexorably back toward the platform

on which Leila stood, the man in black lifted his heavy sword in both hands for a desperate blow.

His foot slipped on the dew-slick weeds and he fell backward, his head striking the edge of the platform.

Volotor knelt on the fallen man's chest, the tip of his sword at his foe's throat. Glancing at Filene, who stood stricken at the edge of the field, the sorcerer nodded toward Leila. "Give her the potion. Then she can plead for him."

Feeling her way across the hazardous ground, followed by Dorma, Filene brought the goblet to the platform.

Leila made no move to take it.

"She doesn't trust you," Dorma told Volotor.

"Why would I harm you?" he asked Leila.

"Considering that you have your sword at the throat of the man who saved her . . ." Dorma murmured.

"Taste it," he told the princess. "Show her it's harmless."

Dorma took the goblet, set down the bird cage, and ascended the platform. She sipped from the potion and handed the goblet to Leila, whispering, "Just a little."

Leila tasted the potion, then handed the chalice to the princess.

"Now, lady, what do you say?" the sorcerer demanded.

"I say you wretched, evil, cruel . . ."

Volotor's hands tightened on the sword hilt.

Dorma stood on the platform above him, holding the goblet. She reached out.

She poured.

The bird cage exploded into splinters, and four tons of dragon appeared upon that field and seized the dripping sorcerer.

As lords and ladies scrambled, screaming, from the stands, the trackers faded into morning sunlight. Dwindling to lizards, the green guards scattered to hide among the weeds.

Blys shook the wizard like a toy. *"I signed a treaty, you know."*

"My love. My noble, valiant . . ." Kneeling beside the man in black, Filene removed his helmet.

"Miles!" Dorma gasped.

"Of course." The sorceress attempted to cradle him in her arms.

"But how did you know?" Dorma asked her.

Filene smiled. "You've never been in love, Princess."

The chimera tethered in the courtyard lifted its head. With a scream that struck terror as far as the village, it spread its dreadful wings, then folded them and stood shivering.

In the stables, Horse disappeared. One moment he was standing in his stall, the next he was simply gone.

Finding himself in a paddock, with no idea how he came to be there, Wincealot shook his head as if to dispel the tatters of some clinging nightmare.

"I haven't been myself lately," he muttered.

twelve

OU are behaving like a beast," Dorma told the dragon. "Swaggering around here like some stupid hero, expecting our constant applause, harassing the chimera, wallowing in the moat, gorging on tea and cakes—when I return from the throne room, I expect to see a sincere change in your attitude."

"Biscuits." The creature lay back, paddling with his tail in the moat as he balanced pastries and teapots on his belly. "On your way back, command the cooks to send me down another half ton of sincere biscuits."

She could not resist kicking a little water at his fiery nostrils before she stalked away.

The overwrought ironwork and fiery urns were gone from the throne room. Wincealot sat on his own unthreatening throne, surveying his weary court.

"You." He turned a regal gaze toward Volotor. "Though your sorcery is dissolved, I have no doubt that you remain a terrible and evil-tempered man. You will be confined for the remainder of your life in the dungeons where you imprisoned our gallant knights and nobles."

Proud and silent, the one-time sorcerer turned away from the king. He glanced at Leila for a moment, hesitated, then followed Wincealot's guards.

"Wait!" she said. "You reckless, willful, wicked man. Is there any hope you could change? Is there any chance you could learn to be reasonable?"

"For you, lady," he said, his voice so low only she heard, "I would have done anything. But now . . ."

She turned to Wincealot. "Sire, if he gives a solemn oath to behave, and I guarantee it, would you pardon him?"

"Never."

"Father," Dorma interposed, "if Leila had drained every drop of that potion, you would still be . . ."

"Not another word!" thundered the king. "I will never pardon him!"

"Never?" Dorma's voice was soft as a mourning dove's, but in her lovely gray eyes was a steely glint.

"Never?" echoed her handmaidens, their voices soft as his daughter's and their gazes as unflinching.

He was reminded of placards and picketing, and a daughter who could not only read but write, and how he might go down in history.

"You would pledge yourself to see he stays reformed?" he asked Leila.

"Absolutely," she assured him.

So the sorcerer was pardoned.

"But I am only an ordinary man now," he told Leila.

"Ordinary? You're fearless, forceful, learned, a master of jousting, running kingdoms . . . and you really know how to handle a chimera."

"So does the Black Knight," he observed, with a trace of bitterness.

"Oh, he's wonderful, but he doesn't want me. And you are incredibly fascinating. What an adventure this will be!"

When Volotor and Leila had gone, Wincealot turned his attention to Filene.

"Sire," she said, "I think you should know that I never dreamed that horse might be the King of Minervia, yourself."

"Thank you. Since my daughter assures me you did once try to help free her, I can't find it in my heart to punish you. If you promise never to practice sorcery again, you're free to leave."

"I'll hardly miss it," she declared.

Finally, the ruler addressed Miles. "What can we say? You defended our child, fought for our kingdom. You don't even have to be census taker anymore. But will you please get that dragon out of the moat?"

"I'm coming with you, love," Filene told the traveler.

"Filene," Miles said, "you'll make the dragon nervous. You make me nervous."

"I have a way with dragons. And while I may have forsaken sorcery, you'll find I can be utterly enchanting."

"Filene, I have been exiled by your brother, hunted by his hawks, trapped by his trackers, nearly done in by his sword. I see no basis for any real relationship between you and me."

"But I've loved you since I was fifteen," she protested. "When Volotor drove you from your land, I would have followed if I'd had any idea where you'd gone. Now that I've found you, what can separate us?"

"Distance," he said, and strode from the throne room.

The Black Knight had been taken to the royal chambers, where Wincealot's own doctors tended him. When Dorma entered, they withdrew tactfully.

"I've missed you," Hugh grumbled. "Where have you been?"

"Negotiating."

"You know what Miles and your uncle did? I'd merely fainted from a few wounds when they took my armor . . ."

"Only because they knew you were hurt too badly to survive a battle with Volotor. Miles very nearly didn't."

138

"Dorma, you and I have things to discuss."

"You still know very little about me, Hugh. I tend to be absentminded. I have my own ideas about how to run a kingdom. I will never touch another tapestry." Then, to her astonishment, she went on, "I am also intelligent and loyal, and have secretly admired you since . . . Filene! That sorceress has put a spell on me!"

She rushed from the chambers. "Filene! You swore no more sorcery!"

Dashing into the council chambers, she demanded, "Where is she? Where is that enchantress?"

"She left," the king said.

"*Left?* Oh."

She hurried back to the Black Knight's side. ". . . admired you since the first time I told you to go away."

In the throne room Wincealot said, "I tell you, her shoes *squish*, as if she'd been kicking in the moat. Arnold, tell me again—you're absolutely sure Hugh is the Black Knight of Doum?"

"Absolutely."

"Do you suppose, if we made him Lord Protector of Minervia, there's a chance we could palm her off on him? We're never going to find a prince foolish enough to marry her—might as well give up on that. It would take years to teach her to sew a decent tapestry and stop bursting into council chambers. But the Black Knight of Doum could stand up to her, maybe even put up with her."

"We were talking about the peace treaty," the high commissioner reminded him.

"Oh. Right. When Doum's ambassador arrives, we'll have a welcoming ceremony, an address by me, then the banquet, a few words from me, the treaty signing, my speech, and, if we work it right, my announcement of Dorma's engagement to Sir Hugh. That should please their prince."

Not so much as a "How was your vacation, dear boy?" Not so much as a "What a ghastly muddle we got ourselves into while you were away, Arnold" or a "You have no idea how desperately we needed you, H.C."

"If it weren't for humans, I could wallow in this moat forever," Blys sighed. "But they're peering at me too much. From the ramparts and palisades and battlements. I can feel it."

"Of course, if you lie around here too long, you'll lose your mystique," Miles observed. "Once they begin taking you for granted, they'll be strolling up to the lair with picnic lunches, misplacing their young among the rocks . . ." He leaped back as the dragon lumbered out of the water.

The lair was still a shambles. After he breathed on a stream to boil water, Blys swept out the worst of the rubble while Miles brewed tea.

"I suppose you could call what I've been through an adventure," the reptile rumbled, flicking Peek Freans biscuit crumbs from his belly, "but it's left me all undone."

"Turned out remarkably well, though, with Hugh recovering and Leila over the shock of the chimera."

"The chimera," the dragon said loftily, "is a mythical beast."

Far below on the path, Filene picked a bouquet of dragonroot, dragonhead, dragonwithe, and other flowers known to appeal to reptiles.

As she worked her way toward the lair, she was smiling.

glossary

basilisk A mythical reptile that could kill with its breath or its glance. Now, a tropical lizard.

battlement A wall along a roof or balcony, with gaps through which to send missiles.

centaur A mythical being with the head and upper torso of a man, the legs and body of a horse.

chimera (ki mere′ a) A mythical monster with a lion's head, a goat's body, and a serpent's tail.

colossus An enormous statue.

Crimea A peninsula in southwest Russia, in the Black Sea.

Cyclops A mythical giant with a single eye in the middle of its forehead.

gargoyle A grotesque carved figure of a human or an animal.

Gorgon Any of three mythical monstrous sisters. Each had wings and claws, and serpents for hair. Anyone looking directly at a Gorgon would be turned to stone.

gryphon (grif′en) Also spelled *griffin*. A mythical monster with the head and wings of an eagle and the body of a lion.

haruspex One who attempts to gain secret knowledge or foretell the future by supernatural means.

joust Single combat between two armored knights on horseback.

knave A dishonest or dishonorable person.

magus (may′jus) One skilled in magic or sorcery.

mead A drink made from water and fermented honey.

newt A kind of salamander.

parapet A defensive wall raised above another wall. A protective wall along the edge of a roof or balcony.

porpentine A porcupine.

rampart A broad elevation built as protection, usually topped with a parapet.

sorcerer One who gains supernatural powers through black magic.

thaumaturge (thŏ′ma turj) One who works wonders.

varlet A low knave, a rascal.

warlock A man who practices black magic.

wench A young woman; a girl.

wimple A cloth covering a woman's head and neck.

whippet A small, fast dog resembling a greyhound.

war platforms Wheeled platforms on which assault towers, catapults, etc., were hauled to the walls of a besieged town or castle.

BEVERLY KELLER shares her home in Davis,
California with five great grizzled dogs.

She "gives us an under-the-skin sense of a kid
alone," said *Kirkus Reviews,* commenting on
Fiona's Flea, the sequel to her first easy-to-read
book, *Fiona's Bee,* which was starred by *Booklist,
Kirkus Reviews,* and *School Library Journal.* Recommending *My Awful Cousin Norbert,* the *Bulletin of the
Center for Children's Books* said, "In a humorous,
lightly and deftly told story, justice prevails."

Beverly Keller has also written *The Beetle Bush,
The Bee Sneeze, The Genuine, Ingenious, Thrift Shop
Genie, Clarissa Mae Bean & Me,* and *The Sea Watch,*
an ALA Notable Book. Her most recent novel for
Lothrop, *No Beasts! No Children!* was named one
of the "Best Books for Spring" by *School Library
Journal.*